SECRETS

SECRETS

by
Constance Lechman

PUBLISHING

(C) 2020 by Constance Lechman

Published by **MERAKI HOUSE PUBLISHING INC.**

All rights reserved. This book or any portion thereof may not be reproduced or used in any manner whatsoever without the express written permission of the publisher except for the use of brief quotations in a book review.

This book is a work of fiction. The characters, incidents, and dialogue are drawn from the author's imagination and are not to be construed as real. Any resemblance to actual events or persons, living or dead, is entirely coincidental.

For any information regarding permission contact
Constance Lechman via

constancelechman@gmail.com

Printed in the United States of America
First publication, 2020.

Paperback ISBN: 978-1-988364-36-0
Ebook: 978-1-988364-37-7

Book cover design by
www.designisreborn.com

DEDICATION

For Jean-Pierre who encouraged me

to write number seven.

ACKNOWLEDGEMENTS

My deep appreciation goes to **Marnie Kay** for her continuing support of my work.

A big thank you to enthusiastic readers **Verna Cuthbert, Sandy Driscoll, Julianna Joos, Bobbi Lechman, Dorothy "Dodo" Macdonald** and **Susan Sand.**

"I was made and meant to look for you and wait for you and become yours forever."

~ **Robert Browning**

"Some day you will find out that there is far more happiness in another's happiness than in your own."

~ **Honoré de Balzac**

"Being deeply loved by someone gives you strength, while loving someone deeply gives you courage."

~ **Lao Tzu**

Chapter One

"The French have the perfect expression for it. They call it *un coup de foudre!* Love at first sight! And that's exactly what it felt like the first time that we met! It was like an unexpected shock that knocked me right off of my feet. A huge quake that shook my whole world. I was completely awestruck and mesmerized the moment that we locked eyes," I say looking at my mentor Melinda Braydon and shaking my head.

"I can still picture that moment in my mind as clearly as the day that it happened, so many years ago!" I murmur grimacing and shrugging my shoulders.

Dr. Melinda Braydon is a senior psychiatrist at our city's largest university hospital complex where we both work in the psychiatry department. She's in charge of the psychiatric emergency service in the hospital's large and busy emergency department. Melinda's about ten years older than me and is very well respected by all of her colleagues and is a sought after psychotherapist with a long waiting list in her private practice. I know that I'm lucky to have her as my colleague and trusted confidante.

I'd called her earlier and asked to see her whenever she could scrape together fifteen minutes. We're sitting in her office in the emergency department sipping green tea from styrofoam cups that I picked up from the small snack bar located near the hospital's main entrance.

I warm both of my hands on the cup as I look around at the familiar surroundings. Her office is small and furnished very sparsely with only the basics; a computer desk with locked drawers on one side, several mismatched chairs and a wall to wall bookcase that reaches the ceiling and is overflowing with professional journals, books and papers. There's a stack of patient charts sitting on top of her desk next to her laptop computer. The pile of charts means that she still has a lot of patients to see today.

She's leaning back in the office style chair behind her desk with her stockinged feet resting in the open bottom desk drawer. Her shoes are laying on the floor next to her desk where she kicked them off as I entered the room and her head is cradled against the padded top of her chair.

"And you? You are definitely the femme fatale, the beautiful enchantress, in this story," Melinda says to me arching her eyebrows. "He must have been swept off his feet when he saw you," she says blowing on the tea and then taking a sip.

"Uh. Yes. I think so," I mutter, crossing my legs at the ankles. "That's what he told me," I mumble as my stomach does a somersault.

"You think so? No, no, no," she says looking at me intently.

Why is this so hard? Melinda won't judge me. She made time in her busy day because I asked for it. That means she cares. She's here for me. I look down at my legs and study my feet. I'm wearing my favourite pair of black leather high heeled pumps. She's right! I know that he liked what he saw. He told me that I was beautiful the first time that he saw me and he never stopped telling me. Well, until recently. The early days were so different from now.

When I met him I had very long dark brown hair. At one point, several years ago, I stopped colouring it and let the grey grow in and cut it short. But as easy as it was to manage the wash and wear style, it made me look so much older. And, although he didn't say anything I knew that Ryan didn't really like it.

Now, I get my hair coloured in a glossy, dark brown shade and it's long enough to hit the top of my shoulders. When I'm at home, I usually wear it in a casual, high ponytail. Ryan used to tease me that I looked like a teenager with my hair like that. I can feel pressure start in my chest at the thought.

Focus, don't get sidetracked by thinking about what used to be. Focus on now! And what is!

I reach around to the back of my head and touch the tortoiseshell hair clip. At work I always have it clipped at the nape of my neck. It looks professional and I think it matches my fashion style which is very simple and understated. Under my hospital lab coat I usually dress in ankle length, tailored slacks and slim fitting skirts and classic styled shirts.

Picturing Ryan and especially that first meeting between us is making it hard for me to speak. Why did I even go there with Melinda? She's looking at me as if she's assessing what I just said.

I feel like I'm holding in my breath, although holding it in is against my will. Because I actually want to breathe. But there's so much pressure on my chest and it's so uncomfortable that it's even an effort to try. I need to move. I can't continue to sit still. I have to move in order to get breathing again.

I recross my legs this time putting one knee over the other. But I'm still suffocating because it's as if I've been holding my breath for a long time. Too long! Too many months. Months? Is it months? Or is it years? I don't know any more, but it's been far too long!

"Why do you say think, Brooke? Look at you. You're gorgeous. Stunning. Don't tell me that your handsome and smart husband Ryan wasn't attracted to you too. And you just said that he told you that," she says smiling and shaking her head at me. "And you've always been such a beautiful looking couple. You must know that! It's important to hold on to those good memories," she says softly.

I blink at her and nod and sigh deeply.

"Everyone always says that about us. And I guess you're right. It's important to focus on the good memories, but I," I manage to say through the pressure and pain in my chest. "But. Well. Now all of that has changed now. And I need you to find me someone. A therapist. Someone very discreet. And it has to be someone that you really trust," I whisper. "I'm a mess right now. I am not an enchanting anything right now. Just a mess! A terrible, terrible mess!"

I feel the tears start to work at the corners of my eyes. There is so much pressure inside my chest that I can barely think let alone take shallow breaths! I run my hand over my chest to try to ease the pressure.

"I'm emotionally, mentally, psychologically and physically exhausted," I slowly gasp out pausing after each word, barely breathing now as the tears start to trickle out of the corners of my eyes and down my cheeks.

Chapter Two

"Lou Grimes," Melinda says, quickly levelling her gaze at me. "It has to be Dr. Lou. He's the best we have in this city," she says in a firm voice while levelling her gaze at me.

"Lou Grimes!" I sputter as my heart starts to beat faster. Lou Grimes! I can't believe that she's suggesting him! It never occurred to me that she would recommend Lou!

Lou's big, 6'3" bulky frame flashes into my mind. He looks more like a former wrestler turned tough private detective than someone who can handle your most fragile feelings. My chest is aching as I picture him. I take a tissue out of my lab coat pocket and dab at the skin around my eye area drying the tears, while I try not to disturb my eye makeup.

"Yes. He's perfect! You don't work directly with him and he's very good. He gets results. You don't need some flake giving you some pat on the back supportive crap. You need a real therapist. I can speak to him for you. If you want. That way you can jump the queue. No pressure. It's entirely up to you," she says and shrugs her shoulders. "Of course, it's got to be your decision and yours only though. Not what I think is best for you or who I recommend!"

I sigh and look at her in the eyes. She stares back at me completely silent. She's right. Lou is known as a man of very few words. So when he speaks, you want to listen. Our colleagues call him the psychiatrist's psychiatrist. A wave of panic floods through my entire body. Dr. Lou Grimes! No! I don't think so! I can't! I don't want him poking around in my deepest, darkest, most private thoughts!

"OK," I quietly mutter looking down at my shoes again. "OK. Go ahead and speak to him. See if he has an opening."

Maybe he'll be too busy to take me on as a patient. I raise my head and look her in the eyes and nod my head slowly. The thought of Lou sitting and doing a mental status on me gives me the shivers. What am I doing saying OK? Why am I telling her to talk to him? What on earth am I getting myself into now? Am I just making my life even worse?

"Trust me, he's the best Brooke. Besides, it's not a life sentence. You can stop if he doesn't help you. No one can help everyone. If it's useless, then you simply stop. What have you got to lose?" she says and takes another sip of her tea.

"In the meantime, I'm curious, where did you and Ryan meet?" she asks me.

I feel another surge of anxiety start to move in the depth of my core. Smile. Don't let her see that you're so uncomfortable. She's probing around. She's good at that. Breathe deeply and smile. Smiles cover everything and even better than that, they can disarm anyone. Maybe even the famous Dr. Lou Grimes! Smiles always distract everyone.

"Secrets. You want me to tell you my secrets," I say, forcing myself to smile and waving my hand as if to push her away.

My underarms are damp and my heart is thumping so hard that I look down to see if I can see my chest jumping.

She waves her hand back and forth in front of her face and laughs.

"Secrets?" Melinda says. "Never! I keep mine. You keep yours. That's my golden rule. Always!"

I take a deep breath and push myself to manage what feels like a very weak smile. I can feel my knees shaking a little.

"Well. We met through a mutual friend. You know, it was set up by a third party. A friend gave him my phone number and we talked very easily on the phone like we were old friends and," I hesitate and sigh. "And we seemed to have so many interests in common that we decided to meet for a date."

I pause and feel a warm glimmer inside that sparks a smile as I picture our initial meeting. I'll never forget it. It is etched deeply into my memory bank as one of the best moments of my entire life. It was a real turning point for me to meet someone in my life who would love me so completely!

"I'll always remember the first time that we saw each other. We had agreed to meet at a local bar for a drink," I say and pause again and brush a strand of hair off of the sleeve of my white lab coat.

"He got there first and he was standing at the bar and he had his back to me and I thought, ugh! He's definitely not my type. Because he looked rigid somehow. I was so disappointed. But then he turned around to see if I was coming and, and well, he saw me and stared into my eyes. I told myself to smile. And I did. I felt his energy change. He softened," I say and stop. "And he never stopped being soft and sweet with me. This big tough guy!" I say tears trickling out of my eyes.

I pick at a tiny piece of fluff on the knee of my black stretch skinny pants as tears start to pour down my face.

"You're holding back," Melinda says softly. "Go on. Get it out!"

I smile again. My stomach is starting to do flip flops. I nod my head at her.

"As I got closer," I say and sigh deeply. "I liked what I saw. A lot. I felt a charge run through my body. You know the way an electric current lights up a lamp when you turn the switch on," I say smiling at the thought.

"It certainly sounds like it was love at first sight," Melinda says softly. "It must be terrible for you now."

I nod my head and smile and take a deep breath to hold the tears back.

"He was so handsome in a very European way. You know, well dressed with a beautiful navy blazer and open neck white shirt. It was all so instantaneous," I say. "A flame ignited deep inside me. And the blaze shot through my body, just as if a match had been struck on a pile of dry kindling," I say snapping my fingers to emphasize my point.

"Just like that!" I whisper, nodding my head at the memory.

"Mmm," Melinda murmurs.

She looks at me as if she's also picturing that moment and is experiencing the way it felt. She puts her elbow up on the edge of the arm of her chair and rests her chin on her hand. She looks sad.

"Thanks. That felt good to remember, Melinda. It felt good. But enough of this. Tell me about how Lou works. What do you know about him, because you know that I've heard he's tough. Relentless, is the word that everyone uses to describe him," I say dabbing at my tears with the now soggy tissue.

"Well, nothing that you don't know. All good therapists work at several different levels at the same time," she says handing me the box of tissues from her desk. "And you know that the patient needs to grasp the fact that the therapist is challenging their defences and their resistance. And as you do in your own practice, your aim like any good therapist, is to give insight into the self-sabotaging behaviour of the patient. And in that way the therapist and patient become partners in a therapeutic alliance to work against that self-defeating part of the patient's psyche," she says quietly. "It's teamwork!"

"Yes, yes," I mumble and nod. "I do know all of that very well. This is my profession. It's my life blood. But to be on the other side of that process. That's something else entirely. I guess I'm scared!"

I whisper.

We stare at each other. I feel my chest start to ache again. How can I let Lou Grimes inside of me? How can I let him see what's really festering inside of me? I just let Melinda in by asking her for help and right now I'm feeling worse. I can't get into something with Lou that's going to make me feel more terrible. It'll be the end of me! I'll never survive it! I can barely breathe now! What will happen when I'm with him and he's probing around inside of me?

"So it's like going into battle against a very powerful, but invisible force that is determined to win against all odds," she continues calmly. "That force; that enemy has a victim and it won't let it go easily. It's like a cat that has caught a mouse and it's holding it under its paw," Melinda says, her voice rising as she ends the sentence.

She takes another sip from the cup of tea and pauses a full minute before speaking.

"So sure he's tough. He has to be strong! But you're tough too. So it will be an even match. You'll see. Just give it everything that you've got and you'll come out as a winner!" she says and purses her lips and flexes her biceps at me.

I swallow hard and nod at her, barely able to take a breath with the burning pressure that's weighing on my chest.

CONSTANCE LECHMAN

Chapter Three

"Chiron the Wounded Healer is in your chart. Look! I can see it in your chart's south node. Look, see? It's right here," the popular astrologer said excitedly.

She pointed to a spot on the astrological chart she'd cast for me and then looked up at my face in order to gauge my reaction.

This was many years ago, when on a whim, well, truthfully, it was when I was a young woman in my first year of university and I was going through a really bad time after a romantic breakup. I'd been badly shaken up after an abrupt end to what I thought was going to be a long-term relationship leading to marriage. I was feeling very unsure of who I was and where I was going in my life. I guess I was looking for a beacon, something to point me in the right direction, so I had my horoscope done by a local astrologer.

Maria was well known in our city as being uncannily right on in her astrological readings and most of my girlfriends had consulted her, when they were feeling at their most vulnerable, especially when in mourning after love affairs had gone wrong.

Chiron? I'd never heard of him or her. I remember staring back at her wondering what all the excitement in her voice and face could be about.

"Chiron signifies that you have deep wounds from a past life, an earlier life. You brought these wounds into your childhood resulting in severe problems in your self image when you were growing up," she explained, peering at me over the red framed reading glasses that were perched on the tip of her nose.

Deep wounds! Self-image problems? I remember how surprised I was when she started telling me this. I wanted to hear if I was going to meet someone else, a Mr. Right! I didn't expect to hear about my childhood. But, I can also recall wanting to hear more, even though a part of me just wanted to run away from all of that hurt.

I haven't thought about that strange encounter for a long time. But it's very fresh in my mind right now. I'm walking home from work carrying a cloth shopping bag of groceries consisting of mostly fresh vegetables and some fruit.

I shop and cook completely differently now. Post-Ryan shopping I call it. Instead of a weekly big shopping trip where I stocked the refrigerator and pantry, I usually stop on my way home to pick up a few things for dinner and to refill the fruit bowl. My fridge and pantry have only a few basic items now, so there's lots of empty space on the shelves.

I no longer make big meals with Ryan's favourite pasta, meat and chicken recipes. He used to sit at the island counter and watch me cook. He always made us a cocktail on Saturday evenings, usually a chilled gin and tonic in the hot summer that easily persuaded me to pause the cooking and sit sipping it with him on our deck. And when autumn came, my favourites, a manhattan or a martini. They were wonderfully warming in the cold winter. Otherwise, it was a glass of wine, usually red. "For our health," he'd say grinning.

Now it's simpler, usually a piece of fish, a cooked vegetable like broccoli and a mixed salad.

And no cocktails to share on Saturdays. Today, I picked up some fresh salmon and a bunch of asparagus along with a bag of some mixed baby romaine greens for a quick salad. I know that I have brown rice at home in the pantry. But I don't have much of an appetite. I need to eat because I'm losing weight. I've always been slim with a good figure, but now my clothes are getting baggy and I'm starting to look too skinny! Hopefully, once I'm at home and I actually start preparing the meal I'll feel more like eating it.

Over the past many weeks without Ryan, I can't keep my mind from wandering back over my life and doing a kind of review. As I arrive at a busy intersection, the light turns red and I stop and wait.

I remind myself to stay alert. I can't be distracted and get hit by a car or a cyclist while absentmindedly stepping off of the curb.

The memory of the astrologer's face floods back into my mind. With the exception of her flashy and very trendy eyeglasses, she was dressed more like a banker than a soothsayer in a navy and white pin striped blouse and navy trousers. The only other non-banker element was the high, yellow laced, black Doc Martens boots she was wearing.

I can remember nodding a lot as she talked. It was eerie that someone who knew nothing about me beforehand, someone whom I'd never even met before, could have so much insight into what seemed to be the very essence of my being.

"Your parents were good parents and you were very attached to them. Your father especially. And he adored you," she'd continued as she touched an area on the chart that she had laid out on the small table in front of us.

While she spoke, she repeatedly pushed her glasses back up onto the bridge of her nose to keep them from sliding down. As she talked about my father, she seemed to gain steam and get more excited.

"Your father doted on you, didn't he?" I remember her asking me with her eyes sparkling.

I can still picture her pushing those glasses back up on her nose and then looking at me waiting for me to respond. But I was paralyzed. At the mention of my father my throat had gone dry and I felt like I couldn't breathe or speak. It's strange, but in a very similar way when I was talking to Melinda earlier today, I was also having a great deal of difficulty breathing. Maybe that's why I'm remembering this encounter with Maria. I had the exact same sensation of suffocating. Obviously, I'm capable of diagnosing myself. And I know that what I experienced earlier today was a panic attack. I haven't had these episodes until recently. That is, until my world was turned upside down because of losing Ryan!

"He used to call me his angel princess," I remember being able to finally whisper to her, although it hurt me to say those words. "He would dance with me. You know in the living room and twirl me around. I can remember that," I'd told her.

"He died young," she said, studying her notes that were stacked on the table next to the chart.

And I'll never forget this as long as I live. She patted her heart with her hand and looked at me.

"His heart," she said.

And how she knew that, I'll never figure out. Because she was right. He dropped dead playing tennis. The autopsy revealed a congenital heart defect that he didn't even know he had! No one knew that he had it until it was too late.

"How old were you? Because obviously you were very young too," she'd continued, pressing me about my father.

Maria was very persistent and it was the first time that I had ever talked about any of this painful part of my past with anyone. I guess I needed to get some of it out because I remember how I answered her.

"He died when I was eleven. Gone. Gone. Just like that. With no warning!" I'd said shocking myself at the words I was using.

My body shudders now at the memory of how he simply disappeared. That great big man. He was tall, well over six feet and broad shouldered and he could pick me up and throw me into the air and catch me like I was a tiny, weightless sparrow. How could he vanish without a trace? He used to crawl on the floor on his hands and knees pretending to be a horse, while I rode on his back. He was my super hero. My very own Superman! My father who I loved so much had just disappeared one day leaving me alone in the world!

"Chiron gives you the patience that you need to sense and to understand the pain of others and in that way it also gives you the power to empathize and heal the pain of those who are suffering. And always remember that as you heal others, you help to heal yourself at the same time!" she told me.

I remember how she looked at me as she slowly emphasized each word. It was a strange, intense mixture of delight and certainty. As if with every word she was slowly unwrapping a very important gift of knowledge that I needed for my life to evolve in not only a successful way, but in the way that it should.

I recall how in those moments I was completely absorbed by her words. Mesmerized! I was unable to speak. I could only nod to her after that for the entire time that was remaining in the session.

So, I guess that it's no accident that I got into the kind of work I do, to help people in severe mental distress. Once I got my medical degree I could have moved on to any number of specialties. I decided on psychiatry and I've devoted years to perfecting my expertise.

Part of my character is my need to work hard. And not only that, I need to do my best. It's a big component of who I am. And I'm really at my best when I'm working with someone who desperately needs my help. I always go the distance. You often hear people say, find something that you're passionate about and do it and then you'll be happy. Well, I'm living proof of that statement. Until now that is. Since I lost Ryan, now even my work feels like a burden at times.

I reach my condo building and the doorman opens the sliding glass doors using a buzzer from his desk by the front entrance. As I get on the elevator, I picture my colleagues. They're all dedicated and we respect each other a great deal. They see me as a very strong and stable person. If they could only see into my mind now they'd be completely shocked!

And all of my friends and neighbours know that they can count on me and they seem to appreciate me for my tough love messages. I'm usually a logical, no nonsense and very common-sense oriented person. Actually, that's another descriptor that everyone uses to describe me. Common sense! And it's true. They're right. Usually! Now my thoughts aren't full of common sense. They're very troubling. Disturbed! They're coming from a very dark place that I've never dared to go before.

I put the bag of groceries down on the kitchen counter and walk into the living room and sit down on the sofa. I take a deep breath.

I am tough, but everyone has their limits. Even me! What others don't seem to realize is how sensitive I am. So sensitive that I can feel when someone is thinking of me or when they've detached emotionally from me. When they no longer are there for me and have left me. They don't have to say a word. I can sense it when they leave me. Emotionally, that is.

I can feel my throat constricting and reflexively I cough a little. The cough helps my chest to release some of the pressure that's been building up inside of me.

I also absorb other people's hurt. That's that damn Chiron again! I absorb the hurt that is inside the people that I love. Sometimes I see into someone, into their eyes and I can see right inside of them. Right into their worst secret selves. Past the exterior, directly into their hurt. And I want to go in there and explore it, take it apart and fix it. I don't care what the hurt is. I only want to help them to bear it.

Of course, every so often I slip, and I make a mistake and when I do it's usually a doozie! And that's what happened with Ryan. I went full throttle, totally optimistic! I was oblivious, when I should have taken the time to see what was really happening with him. I should have seen the signs. Why didn't I? I guess I saw only what I wanted to see. I was in full denial.

When I think of him I don't picture his face or his body. I picture his eyes. I see the magnet drawing me into the deep tunnel of his inner self, into his soul. And I can't bear the pain of losing him anymore

That's why I might need some time out right now. To recharge. To restore myself. My inner being needs healing. Maybe that's why I do need a psychiatrist, even though I really don't want to go to see Lou Grimes. How will I be able to let him help me while I'm still hanging on to my deepest secret? How can I tell him everything? I bury my head in my hands and sob uncontrollably.

Chapter Four

"Now I really need your help to be able to forgive Ryan for leaving me! I know that sounds terrible when I say that but I, I can't help it," I stammer to Melinda as I blow my nose with a wadded up tissue and swipe at the tears that are seeping down my cheeks. "Why? Why is he leaving me like this? I can't believe it. I never in a million years would have expected this!" I wipe more tears from my cheeks with the back of my hand. "We had a deal," I say squeezing the phone in my hand as hard as I can as a shock runs up and down my spine.

"A deal?" Melinda says quickly.

Oh no! Why did I say that? It just popped out! I shocked myself when I heard it come out! I'm sitting alone in my living room, but I nod my head at her question and wipe my eyes again. My hand is holding the phone so tightly that it begins to hurt so I consciously try to relax my grip on the phone and carefully switch hands.

"Not to, not, you know to never ever leave each other. You know, never to let the other one suffer in any way. That was our deal! And he was the one who initiated it and he was the one who insisted on it!" I say my voice rising to a shriek.

"I see," Melinda says. "Well you can never predict the future. You know that. And from what you've said and also from what I've seen of the two of you, you have had a great marriage up until now. Isn't that true? I'm sorry. I know that sounds trite. I know my saying that to you doesn't help your despair about what's happened," she says.

I take a deep sigh and nod my head. She's right. We did have a great marriage. That's why this is so hard to take. If we'd fought and argued, then maybe it wouldn't be so bad right now to be so alone. I'd probably be relieved.

"You don't have to apologize Melinda. You're absolutely right. We had a great marriage. It's me. I had no idea that I was living in a life with a future that was so full of such terrible things to come," I say and shake my head. "What signs did I miss to end up in this kind of mess? Why didn't I see it sooner and do something to change it? I'm a doctor damn it! A trained professional. What's wrong with me? I should have prevented this. In some way! I should have been able to see the symptoms and do something about it!"

"Nothing. There's nothing wrong with you. And you're a good doctor. But you're not clairvoyant. You can't foresee the future. So you assumed that you and Ryan were OK forever, just as anyone would," Melinda says. "You can't control everything in this world just because you're a doctor and you can't control everyone else and everything that happens to you or them in life. None of us can control the future. Hell! We can barely control the present moment."

I nod again. Not clairvoyant. She's right. But obviously a wounded healer! I can hear her breathing through the phone while she pauses waiting for me to speak. Hearing her breathe brings tears to my eyes again. I miss Ryan so much. I loved laying against his chest at night in bed listening to his heartbeat in my ear. Tears trickle down my neck.

"I'm so alone now. The thing is that I don't need someone to look after me. I just want someone to love me. Me. Me for me. For who I am. Ryan has always done that! I want him back with me. He's always been my rock. So sweet and so strong at the same time. My brave, strong man! I don't need Lou Grimes to tell me that he replaced my father as the man in my life," I snap.

"I can't tell you that the future will be alright Brooke. But you'll somehow find the strength to get through this. I know you and you will be able to draw on your inner resources to do just that," Melinda says speaking in such a soft voice that it feels like her words are gently stroking me as she talks. "In the meantime, it will do you some good to talk to Lou Grimes. It can't hurt. Can it?"

"True. True, I guess it's true. Thanks. You're right. Thank you. I'll keep in touch," I say ending the call and putting my cell phone down on the sofa next to me.

I look around the spacious living room. I'm lying on an art deco sofa. Ryan and I bought it together at a Sotheby's auction along with two matching occasional chairs in a deep amethyst velvet upholstery. We got them years ago, but we recently had them recovered in the original jewel toned colour. I stroke the soft velour of the sofa.

Several large black and white photographs of our travels, in gold frames, decorate the pale, ivory coloured walls of the living room. The photographs were taken by Ryan who absolutely loves photography! It's always been his baby. He especially loved taking photos on our many vacations in southern Italy!

Soon after we were married, we found out that we couldn't have children. I truly think that taking photos and developing them into beautiful pieces of art was his way of fulfilling his need for creating and nurturing. As a result, he has become a very good amateur photographer. Well, I guess that's in the past now too! A whimper escapes as I picture him with his camera, always with a big grin on his face.

In front of the sofa there's a Carrara marble top, brass trimmed, circular coffee table. Matching marble topped end tables sit beside the plush chairs.

Before we moved into the three bedroom, three bathroom unit, we installed new wide plank, dark oak floors. They're a striking contrast to the airy and bright spacious condo with lots of south facing windows and high ceilings that are trimmed with elegant, white ogee crown moulding.

Ryan and I each took a bedroom to use as an at home office space. Ryan's has been part office and part photography studio. I closed the door and haven't reopened it since he left. I know that eventually I'll need to think about what I'll do about that room now. My heart starts to pound and I feel like I can't breathe. I stand up and walk in circles taking deep breaths, pushing my shoulders back, to try to open up my chest to let in some air.

These panic attacks are becoming more and more frequent. The first time that I remember not being able to breathe was immediately after my father died. Now I'm having attacks at home and sometimes even at work. What did Maria the astrologer say so long ago? That I brought wounds into this life with me? Did I? I just know that as a child I was crying and missing my father and I was terribly sad. After he died, I destroyed my favourite doll and my mother scolded me and told me that she didn't want me to be angry. Angry? I guess I was. But, I was also ashamed! I was embarrassed! I had bragged about my father, my idol, to all my friends and now he was gone!

"Embarrassed?" I mumble out loud. "Why? Because he never came back!" I say frowning. "Embarrassed, because he never even came back to say goodbye to me!"

As I repeat the word embarrassed my mind is charged with energy! Obviously, when I was a child, I had the idea that somehow I was humiliated by his death. That in some way when I lost him, when he left me, my deep attachment and love for him became a source of humiliation! I was no longer any good! If I was better, he would have never left me!

I've never thought of it in this way until right now! No wonder I tried to buffer my feelings as a teenager and continued to do so as an adult until Ryan came along, and then I let them run free again and I got very attached to him. Now I've closed up again and it's been suffocating me!

The pain in my chest has disappeared. I'm breathing easier. I feel tired. Not the restless toss and turn all night kind of tired, but the deep restful kind of tired that I desperately need in order to sleep tonight.

Chapter Five

"I love you sweetie," I murmur into Ryan's ear.

He's sitting on a small sofa quiet, not moving. Too still. I'm cuddled up next to him. I shouldn't be, but I want to hear him breathing and I want to be able to feel his heart beating against my body. It's eerie because he's very, very still. No longer responding to me or to my touch. He's no longer here for me! I feel the tears start in the corners of my eyes. The thought of him not responding to my touch is unbearable. My heart actually aches right now. I put my hand over it and rub gently to ease the hurt.

I softly stroke his face. My husband. My beautiful, handsome husband. No matter what happens he'll always be my husband. I'll be married to him forever, for eternity. Even though he's leaving me, he'll always be my only true love. Others may replace me in his world. But, no one can ever replace him in my life.

I love to touch him. Tenderly, softly, slowly. It's heaven to run my fingers over his face to try to show him that I still love him. No matter what is happening to us, I want him to know that I can still love him. I need to hang on to that.

Ryan had a loving, early family life and he has lived his whole life in the same way. Because of that beginning, he has always been as lovable as he can be to everyone he encounters. Now, he isn't giving any love to me to fill the hole that he's creating. He can no longer make up for that terrible early, emotional loss of my father that goes right to the centre of my soul and traumatizes and overwhelms me. The loss is so deep seated that it can only be healed from the inside out.

As a psychiatrist and a doctor I know that I'm fooling myself if I think that my deep love for Ryan could ever completely cure that kind of core deficit.

However, Ryan's nature has pushed me out of my comfort zone and over time I've become a much more openly affectionate and emotionally demonstrative mate. So that's been good for me. And of course for him too! It's worked both ways!

My amazing husband Ryan, The Ryan Adams, as he is referred to by his clients, is a sixty year old corporate lawyer, who is a senior partner in the top law firm in our city. He's a tough minded scorpio, a horoscope sign that is very compatible with mine.

He's tall, 6'1" with grey streaked, dark brown hair and bluish grey eyes. He has a salt and pepper Keanu Reeves style beard and wears black framed glasses that give him an elegant, but business-like air. All in all he looks like a take no prisoners kind of senior executive from central casting.

I love his voice. It's a deep, sexy masculine voice that adds to his commanding presence. He's extremely articulate and selects his words carefully. I guess that caution is part of being a lawyer.

His sophistication is a big part of what attracted me to him. He is utterly refined in his taste in clothing, furniture, art and travel. And we're both very knowledgeable about food and wine from all of our extensive traveling to Europe and Asia.

Despite a hectic law career, Ryan has always found time to attend the monthly presentations and viewings at his photography club and to work out several times a week at a private gym.

Thanks to Ryan's professional success and resulting lucrative financial reward, we live in a much sought after high security downtown condo building that is close enough that we can both walk to our offices. It's also handy to bike paths and Ryan loved to ride his bike every weekend with a couple of his lawyer friends.

"Everything is easy with you," he said to me a few weeks after we first met.

"I know, I feel the same way about you," I remember answering. "Talking, being together. It's amazing. So comfortable. It's as if we've always been together. We are like one person," I'd said smiling and touching his cheek with my fingertips. I remember the feel of the soft texture of his beard.

"Brooke and Ryan. That's us. Together forever. Just like we are right now at this moment," I'd added, handing him the bottle of wine that we'd just selected to try.

I can remember as if it just happened a moment ago how he opened the drawer and took out the corkscrew and opened the bottle, while I found the glasses in the cupboard. Symmetry. No thinking or pre-planning involved. Smooth like a well practiced team, right from the beginning. I smile as I replay the scene in my mind.

I remember the first time that we made love. We were out for dinner. The memory is as clear as a cloudless blue sky. It was our sixth time together. I had counted the number of dates we'd had before we met that evening. It was his birthday. And we went out for dinner to celebrate. During our tiramisu dessert he leaned over and whispered in my ear, "I want to make love to you tonight."

Electricity runs up and down my spine at the memory. Picturing it now it's as if I'm back there with him in the restaurant. I remember looking at him and saying, "OK. I'd like that. But, I'm nervous."

"Nervous? Why? You don't need to be frightened," he'd said, smiling as he touched the hair on my temple.

"I don't want you to think that I'm a bumbling idiot," I'd slowly muttered in a barely audible voice. "I want to be sexy for you and attractive."

"Bumbling? Impossible. Never. You're my beautiful half. We fit together. Absolutely perfectly together and let's always stay together and love each other," he'd whispered into my ear. "Let's make a deal," he'd said smiling. "We'll never leave each other and we'll never let each other suffer. Not in any way. Ever! Our secret pact! Deal?" he'd repeated, as he held out his hand to shake mine.

"Deal," I'd said as he grasped my and we solemnly shook on it.

He then reached into his blazer and took out his wallet and pulled out a twenty dollar bill as I watched him wondering what he was doing.

"I'm a lawyer and that's a contract," he'd said pressing the money into my hand and closing my fist over it. "There! Money has been exchanged. That seals the deal!" he'd said smiling.

He then pulled me into him and hugged me and lightly kissed me on the lips. I shiver at the memory. Our deal! We can't go back on a deal! Right? A deal is a deal! Isn't it?

Chapter Six

"Shit! Damn it!" I blurt out after cutting my index finger.

I turn to the kitchen faucet and run the cold water over the wound until it stops bleeding. I pull a paper towel off the roll and wrap it around my finger and press on the wound.

"Damn it!" I say pounding my other hand down on the counter.

I never cut myself. I know how to properly handle a chef's knife. I don't need this right now! I feel the tears starting and the turmoil in my stomach increasing. I sit down on one of the island stools and focus on taking some deep breaths.

My kitchen has always been my sanctuary and my creative place, where I can cook and relax. I've always told everyone that cooking is like a form of meditation for me. I lose myself and my worries disappear as I focus on transforming the ingredients.

I continue pressing on the cut as I look around me. Before we moved in Ryan had the kitchen renovated and spared no cost hiring the city's top rated interior designer. He said that he wanted it to be my dream space. He had his studio and he wanted to give me my own special spot too!

And he did! It's all white and spacious, with a huge food pantry, lots of cabinetry for storage including a small appliance garage and white Carrara marble countertops patterned with soft grey veining. We have a huge, eye-popping nine foot centre island. The backsplash is tiled with a gorgeous light, silvery grey arabesque design that sets off the extra large stainless steel fridge with French doors and the commanding presence of the six burner gas stove complete with a pot filler.

Next to the kitchen there's another room that functions as a large butler's pantry with it's own sink, second dishwasher and fridge. It's pure luxury! And an entertainer's dream. We've hosted lots of cocktail and dinner parties for friends and colleagues and it's been wonderful to have all of this space.

Damn! Why did I have to cut myself? I'm a better cook than that. I need to pay more attention to what I'm doing! Right now I'm chopping onion and garlic for a tomato and fresh basil pasta sauce. That has to be my focus. Nothing else! I have to be more careful and stop thinking about the past. I need to change what I'm doing and start to do things differently from now on. I have to focus my attention. I need to keep the focus on what I'm doing at the moment, and not on what has happened to me and Ryan.

I especially need to stop thinking about how much I want to express my love to Ryan. He was always such a loving, happy go lucky guy who could take my affection and enjoy it, because he knew how much I loved him. He comes from a big, lively happy family and so when we met and connected so strongly he appreciated what it was like to be loved by me. He already knew what it felt like to be treated with tenderness and affection. So he could accept everything I had that was stored up for so long and needed to give to him.

In that way, his background is very different from mine. Losing my father killed whatever love was left in my mother. After she lost my brother and then my father she lost her interest in life itself! And in me. The only good thing about that was the time I got to pet sit little Spiky, my neighbour's fifteen pound mixed breed mutt. He was usually left alone in the yard and when I passed by I always stopped to talk to him and pet him through the fence. One day the neighbour asked my mother if I could take care of him while they went on a week long summer vacation. I held my breath. Miraculously, my mother agreed, mostly because I don't think she had the mental energy to think about it and decide anything else.

Spiky and I were in heaven. He loved it when I scratched his fat little tummy. We played all day and slept every night, cuddled together in my bed. All in all, except for Spiky, it was not a great loving, secure start to my life!

I know that because of Ryan's affectionate and demonstrative nature I was drawn to him like the proverbial moth to a blazing flame. Now I have to live on the smoke and fumes. Maybe it will be OK. Hope keeps me going. Does that make me weak or just stupid? Denial! Obviously denial! I don't know and I don't care, I just keep wanting him back again. It's a craving that comes from so deep within me that I can't ignore it. And it won't go away. It gnaws at me continually.

Today, when I stopped at the grocery store on my way home from work. I overheard two shoppers talking in the supermarket cashier line. One of the women who was about fifty years old, was saying that she sends her husband emoji kisses in her texts when he is away on business. The other one, much younger, said she does the same thing with her new boyfriend every night. I had to push back the tears as I listened to them.

How lucky they are! Two active partners sending and receiving affectionate messages, even if it's in a text. It's still wonderful! I wish!

So now I am building some body armour to protect me from feeling. It's become so much easier to see everything from the outside, rather than feeling it from the inside which just hurts me.

Maybe that's another reason why I became a psychiatrist in the first place. I can focus on the pain of others and not have to feel my own sadness and despair. I guess that has also been my saviour until now. Maybe that astrologer was right after all. I'm really just a wounded healer!

It's clear that at some point, most probably when my father left me, I decided unconsciously to become an observer of life. Not to live my emotional life in any way, not to experience it first hand. Rather only to observe it. From a distance. It makes it so much easier to deal with pain that way. There's no more feeling any deep, excruciating agony. When Ryan came along, then everything inside of me changed! I did a flip flop. Not immediately. But slowly, gradually. And I became an emotional, feeling person. So now I need to change back and consciously return to using the armour!

And I really need to ratchet it up now. I let myself slip with Ryan because of his loving character. I thought life would be wonderful forever! Why hadn't I increased the detachment before this and been more wary? Why should I let myself suffer even a little because of him? And why should I continue to suffer? When I can just step back and observe and go back to not feeling my life.

Most of all, I now need to watch this life of mine unfold. Not try to change or alter it in any way. Will it eventually be in my favour? I will simply follow life and watch what happens. I won't let it dominate me. Never again. I will just go along for the ride. I won't actually try to drive and control the direction of where it's going any more.

Observing. Absorbing. Buffering. Observing so I don't feel the pain, but the pain has to go somewhere. I think Einstein proved that, didn't he? Energy just doesn't disappear. So it gets absorbed, inside, into my body. And buffered by being the observer not the recipient. It's circular. It requires all three components and that's how it works best. Simple really!

Why did this have to happen to us? What's going on and why is it happening? To us! To us! I won't hear him whisper into my ear ever again. He won't touch me again. Ever! Stop! Stop thinking that way right now! Observe remember? Observe. I slow the word down in my mind as I repeat it to myself. I draw it out slowly, picturing the letters. No judging any more. No prejudging. No wondering why, where, or how it happened. I must simply live and observe my life as if it is happening to someone else. I feel my breathing slow down and my heart beat slower. I'm relaxing. My mind is clearing. The panic has subsided. I take a deep breath.

Chapter Seven

"You have to open your heart if you want to write a new story, one that smacks of real life, especially a nice, juicy love story," my best friend Kylie emphasizes as she opens two packets of raw sugar and shakes both of them into her cup of cappuccino.

I've never seen her use sugar before, let alone two packets. I stare at her. My mind starts to whirl. What if I can't open my heart ever again? What if it has too much scar tissue? Doesn't scar tissue have to be surgically excised? Shouldn't it be cut away for new healthy growth to occur?

We're sitting in a new café that's just opened in our neighbourhood. The decor is modern with white walls and square, wooden topped, bar style tables with straight chrome legs. The chairs are a simple linear design also with chrome legs and they're upholstered in a light grey fabric. There are three sleek, navy blue velvet sofas scattered throughout the café. They provide the only depth of colour in the room.

I sigh and stare at her. I guess Kylie should know. She's now a best selling author. She had the confidence to believe in herself and start writing late at night while she was working as a family physician. Now she's writing full time and making oodles more money than she did as a doctor.

Kylie's one of those natural beauties with chin length curly blonde, sun-streaked hair. She gets away with a minimum of makeup. Some navy blue eyeliner and dark brown mascara with a light coral lipstick. Effortlessly, she dresses in a comfortable, but classy put together way. Usually, she's dressed like a fashion model in the latest styles, but today I note that she's wearing baggy jeans with a wrinkled white shirt that looks like it was pulled out of the laundry basket. The only fashionable part of her outfit are the grey snakeskin, mid-heeled ankle boots that she's sporting.

"What do you think?" she says to me while she scans the room.

"I guess you're right. I mean, I think I know what you mean about being open to starting a new life," I say sighing.

"Not that" she snaps. "I meant, what do you think about this place? Do you like it?" she says, continuing to look around the spacious cyber café.

I look around, taking in the sparsely decorated white walled decor.

"The cappuccino looks good," I say as I pick up a spoon and swirl the foamy dome of milk into the coffee in my cup. "And the navy sofas are pretty. But it seems so bare somehow. And it's not the warmest ambience is it?"

"Understatement," Kylie says, shaking her finger at me as she throws her head back and laughs.

We met in university as undergraduate students and we went to medical school together. I chose a specialty in psychiatry and Kylie decided to become a general practitioner. She used to say to me that she looked at the whole patient, not just one of their body parts. She'd tell me that I could shrink the heads, but there'd be no organ management for her. She'd deal with the whole body.

We've also been a part of a friend's circle that meets every Thursday evening for after work drinks and nibbles in one of the bars or restaurants that are close to my office at the hospital. Occasionally, she and I also meet for lunch or coffee on the weekend. Today we'd decided to meet and try out this new café that opened a couple of weeks ago.

"They didn't overdo the decor. And it's not like the service is that great or the coffee is anything to write home about," Kylie snipes, her gaze skittering over our surroundings.

We both burst out laughing.

"For a different generation. Not us," I say nodding at the iPad wielding server who is circling the room and is now walking over to take coffee orders from a newly arrived young couple.

"Everything is online now, even getting an order of cappuccino," Kylie says shaking her head. "What was wrong with placing an order at a counter or giving it to a waiter with a menu and a pad and pen in his hand?" she says and shrugs her shoulders and giggles.

"How's your new book going?" I ask her.

"OK! It's at that point where I'm putting pieces of the plot together in my mind so that it all makes sense. Writing is tough at times. Especially at the beginning of a new book. I need to be patient and go slowly so the characters can grow and develop. Then they tell me their story. I can't push it you know! And it only starts making sense to me when I listen to the characters, no matter what they say.

So I'm at a point now where it's starting to really come together for me. It's exciting!" she says grinning widely and looking at me in the eyes for the first time since we sat down.

"It sounds a little confusing as well as exciting. And I'm sure that you're making it sound easier than it actually is," I say smiling. "Because you've got the secret sauce. Your books are a real success."

"Secret sauce sounds good. But, yes on both points," she says and takes a sip of her coffee. "It's a lot of hard work. It's a good thing that I love doing it. It's just that well right now, I'm a little tired so maybe I'll take a break for a while. Who knows," she says and hesitates and her whole body seems to slow down. "Life is strange. Now I write books that other people read to escape from their life. And before, as a child and as a teenager, I escaped from life by diving into books and reading for hours on end. It's a complete 360 degree turnaround. But it's still my escape hatch, I guess. Maybe that's why I like it so much. It's a legitimate escape. You can't get arrested for it," she says and laughs putting her hand over her mouth and shaking her head at me.

I stare at her. She seems restless and she's laughing so loudly that other patrons are looking our way.

"And you Brooke? How's work? Oops, just a sec," she says holding up her hand.

She pulls her cell phone out of her pants pocket and shakes her head as she looks at the screen. As I watch her I notice that she has dark circles under her eyes that I've never seen before. She must be burning the midnight oil writing that new novel. No wonder she says that she's tired.

"Sorry. It's my sister texting me to say that everything went OK at the doctor today. Thank goodness because I was really worried about her!" she says putting the phone down on the table.

I see tears form in her eyes, while my stomach starts to do flip flops at the mention of her sister. I can feel heat rising in me, threatening to burn my cheeks. I need to control myself. I clear my throat.

"That is good news. I'm sure that you were very worried about her," I say, my fingers tightening around the handle of my cup. I'm aware that I'm clenching and unclenching my left fist under the table.

"I love her so much. I don't know what I'd do if anything happened to her," Kylie says with tears still shining in her eyes.

My heart sinks listening to her. I nod and force myself to smile. I swallow to try to ease the lump in my throat. All this stuff with Ryan has made me so vulnerable!

"You're lucky to have a sister like that," I say aware that my voice sounds a little hoarse.

Why am I reacting so strongly? After all these years. What's happened with Ryan has really shaken me to my very core. As I sit staring at my coffee cup I can feel my heart pumping.

"Do you miss having a sister Brooke?" Kylie asks, wiping the tears from her cheeks with the back of her hand.

"No, no of course not," I say, forcing a smile. "No. No sibling problems. No competition," I say smiling wider. "It's all good," I say feeling the beads of perspiration on my forehead.

Chapter Eight

"When I hug you, I hug you so tightly that I feel like I'm reaching in and touching your soul. I don't know where that comes from. I've never hugged anyone like that before," I whisper to Ryan with my lips against his cheek.

This may be the last time that I can touch him like this. Who knows? I can't see into the future. Right now the present is even completely bleak. I want to savour this moment with him. Now, every contact may be my last. I snuggle in closer against his body.

I love the feel of his beard against my lips. It's such a wonderful mixture of softness and roughness. I reach up to brush my fingertips against his cheekbone. I run my hand over his chest. Ryan looks down at me and my eyes lock on to his. It feels like old times, like we're young again and time is standing still.

I'm laying next to him on top of the bed. We're both fully clothed except for our shoes. When I entered the room and saw him lying on the bed I kicked my shoes off and laid down next to him. He's beautifully dressed as always in a white shirt, a blue wool blazer that has a fine brown stripe in a window pane pattern and fashionable black denim jeans. His shoulders and chest still look strong and powerful even though he's going to be sixty years old in a few months.

His classic looks and European style of dressing have always taken my breath away. Just looking at him can bring me to my knees. How could any man be so handsome? Ryan's still the best looking man that I've ever seen. How could I have been so lucky to meet him? And how is it possible that he could have chosen me to marry?

I run my hands through his hair. It's silky soft. I'm always amazed by how soft it feels because it's wavy and it looks as if it would be wiry to the touch. It reminds me of Willy, my neighbour's rescue mutt. He has very wiry looking fur, but it's velvety soft to the touch.

Ryan always teased me that Willy was his biggest competitor. "You love him more than me," he'd say, pretending to pout and then smiling from ear to ear. "It's true," I'd tell him. "I do love that sweet, little guy an awful lot," I'd say giggling at him.

The first time Ryan ever scared me and truthfully the first time that I was really angry at him was when he was in an accident with his bicycle. It infuriated me when I learned that he'd been riding his bike in a busy traffic area and without his helmet. He'd promised me that he would always wear a helmet even though he hated it. And he swore that he'd be very careful of traffic!

Witnesses told the police that he was going straight at a busy intersection in rush hour traffic and a car that was turning right hit him. He was thrown into the air and landed head first on the pavement and then bounced! It's sickening to think about it. The driver just walked away after telling the police that he didn't see him in his blind spot!

That was the first time that I had to face the possibility of losing Ryan! I feel the rage move inside of me.

I'll never forget that phone call from the hospital trauma centre telling me that he was in the ICU with a head wound, a severe concussion and a broken shoulder and pelvis. I was shaking so badly when I got the call that I could barely stand. I called my neighbour and thankfully she drove me to the hospital. I cried the whole way there.

A traumatic brain injury is what the ICU doctor kept repeating to me as I stood there staring at a barely recognizable Ryan. The only part of his head that wasn't bandaged was a badly bruised black and purple face, so swollen that I couldn't believe that it was him. He was hooked up to two monitors and intravenous tubing. I remember trying to comprehend what the doctor was really telling me. But I was so frightened that I couldn't move. And I could barely absorb the facts. I was convinced at that moment that I was going to lose my husband even though the surgeon kept reassuring me that he was going to live.

Despite the reassurance from the hospital staff I knew when I saw how terribly broken he was in that hospital bed that things would never be the same. He might have cheated death, but he might also change and never be the same Ryan. I hoped against hope that my faithful companion might live, but I couldn't foresee that he might recover and still leave me!

I run my hands under his shirt collar and down the back of his neck. I inhale sharply as I feel the cool smoothness of his skin. I sigh deeply as I move my lips against his neck. I want to take him in. I want it to be just him and me. Again. No problems. Just us. I want Ryan to make love to me again, just like before. I sigh deeply because I know that he won't.

How dare he leave me! How could he? Tears start to stream down my face and drop on to my neck. I shudder as I weep. Why am I crying? I know that I'm angry. I can feel the heat of the anger inside of me! I'm really mad! Enraged! Completely enraged. I feel the powerful force inside of me that wants to strike out and get even! Get my life back! I want to break everything until it's fixed again.

But to kill him instead! No! Never. Never. Never! I'm a doctor. Obviously, I know how to do it. But I took an oath to heal and to do no harm! I'll kill myself first. That would be easier and better! Oh my God! Help me! I'm losing it! I'm going crazy! Insane! I feel a tear slowly slip down my cheek.

Chapter Nine

"Good morning Dr. Adams. Please, come in and have a seat," Lou Grimes says to me indicating the dark brown chair across from where he is standing.

The chair is an exact twin of the leather club chair that he is standing beside. It's angled in front of his desk. It's the patient's chair. He will sit in the doctor's chair. I'm a patient here. He might address me as doctor, but I'm not one here. Here, he is the doctor.

"Thank you," I say through lips that suddenly feel very thick.

My mouth is dry and my knees are trembling slightly. Grow up! You're fifty-three years old. You're not a child. And he's not the big, bad wolf. He's a professional. A therapist. Like you, my inner voice reminds me as my stomach clenches.

Dr. Grimes is a tall, broad-shouldered, rugged and tough looking, but still handsome man in his early sixties with thick, salt and pepper hair and an olive complexion. He has brown eyes with noticeable green flecks that I would under other circumstances find very attractive. Right now they're penetrating me, looking right through me and they're responsible for orchestrating the acrobatics in my core. Is he a Chiron? No, I don't think so. No wounds there. Only confidence and sure-footedness.

He's wearing dark brown dress pants and a pale blue shirt with the sleeves rolled up to his elbows. He looks like he's ready to go to work. On me!

I swallow and look around his office. My eyes focus on the floor to ceiling dark wood bookcases crammed with professional books and journals. He's very neat. Even his desk, which is large and imposing and also made from dark wood, is neat and tidy. There's just a sleek, closed laptop and a landline on one side. I can also see a cell phone sitting next to the laptop. And on the other side there's a desk lamp. It's one of those brass, banker style lamps with the traditional bright green shade.

As I sit down, my eyes continue to scan and I spot a notepad with a pen sitting on top, close to the edge of his desk and within reach of where he's sitting. What kind of notes will he write about me? Will he label me a neurotic, or maybe a character disorder? With depression and anxiety?

"Would you like to tell me how I can help you," he says as he sits down across from me.

I turn to look at him. He is staring straight into my eyes. My mouth feels so dry that I swallow twice before I can even attempt to speak.

"I. I uh," I mumble and move my eyes away from him and over to the window behind his desk.

It's a grey day outside with a brisk, cool breeze. There's a tree outside his window. A big tree. And its branches are swaying in the wind. It's the kind of window that you can open wide and let in the air. But not today. It's too chilly to do that. I shiver slightly.

Aside from the window, the only lighting comes from two lamps, the one on his desk and another on a side table close to our chairs. It gives the office a somber, professional kind of ambience.

I can feel him still staring at me. How did I get here? I'm supposed to be asking the patient how I can help them. I'm supposed to be in the driver's seat. In full control.

"I think I need to speak to someone," I manage to say.

My heart is pounding in my chest. I can hear it in my ears and it's drowning out my voice. I put my hand over my heart to soothe it.

"Why me? A psychiatrist. You must have had a reason to come here today to consult me," I hear him say.

It's as if he's very far away and his voice is in some kind of a sound tunnel. It's faint. Very faint in the distance somewhere very far away.

"Hmm," I hear him say.

"I. Yes. Yes. I need ...some uh help," I respond and burst into tears.

I rummage in my purse for a packet of tissues and pull two out to blot under my eyes and blow my nose. He waits silently while I compose myself. I wad the wet tissue in my hand, close my fist on it and look at him.

"How can I help you?" he repeats emphasizing the word I.

He never seems to move. His bulky frame fits snugly in the chair. His feet are planted on the cherry red Persian style rug. His voice is steady. He looks like he'll wait forever if he has to for me to answer him. Stubborn. Stubborn and sure of himself.

I'm trapped! Like a bug caught in a jar. Why did we do that as kids? It was so cruel. Why didn't we see how cruel we were when we trapped them? Inevitably they died from lack of oxygen.

I take a deep breath to try to extinguish the rush of anxiety that erupts inside my core. My mind is racing with thoughts tripping over themselves. I can't escape. I have no choice. I'll have to tell him. I'll have to expose the pain. He won't accept anything less. I see that. This man won't accept anything less from me. The lump in my throat grows so big that I can barely breathe.

"There's. W-well, I uh...I had a twin, a brother and, and .. and he. He's nonexistent. in my life. I mean. He died, really," I stammer.

Why the hell did I say that? Why am I telling him that shit? Because he's a bloody psychiatrist and

I'm a patient? I have to blurt that shit out! As if that must be the root cause of all of my problems? That's too stupid!

"He died? When did your brother die?" he says and his right eyebrow lifts slightly as he speaks.

He doesn't believe me! He's not going to buy any shit from me. He wants me to get down to it. He wants to go to the core of my sadness.

"A. A long time ago. You see. It. It was many years ago, not long after, right after we were, you know, born," I stammer out the words in a barely audible voice.

He shifts slightly in his chair and waits. He has the most intense eyes that I've ever encountered. They seem to be able to see right through me, right into my feelings and worse, right into my most intimate thought processes. My pulse is racing and my heart is pounding. I feel the tears moving into my eyes and I blink them back. I know that I can't continue to hide in my tears. No longer. I have to face all of this. Finally!

But I have to be careful. Whatever I do I can't slip and tell him everything. Just in case. No one can know everything. No one can ever suspect anything. Some thoughts will have to remain my secret. Forever!

I take a deep breath. I turn my head slightly and scan the spines of the books in the bookcase. *Psychodynamic Psychotherapy, Transference Neurosis. The Standard Edition of the Complete*

Psychological Works of Sigmund Freud. It's a leather-bound set. Freud? What would Freud say about me? Would he say that I am a hysteric?

"Are you here because of your brother?" he says in a voice that commands me to turn back and look at him.

"I uh. My um ...my brother. I don't know," I say looking down at my hands. "No. No. But I do need to deal with it. At some point I need to deal with it. Obviously it's a long time ago. I think it damaged me a lot though," I mumble and look up at him.

"That's intellectual. Theoretical. Does that help you? Being intellectual? You're an intelligent woman and you're a psychiatrist. Does that help you to intellectualize about your problem, about your brother?"

My stomach churns. What an asshole! How dare he talk to me like that! Who the hell does he think he is?

"Does it?" he persists in a steady, even tone.

I take a deep breath and stare at his tie.

"No. I guess not. I mean no. It hasn't helped me. Not so far," I whisper in a barely audible voice.

Damn him! I need to escape as fast as I possibly can! Just get the hell out of here. And never ever come back. This is way too dangerous for me! Every time I speak I get in deeper. He knows that I'm a fraud right now. He can see right through me, right into the dark vault where I keep my terrible secret thoughts and feelings.

Chapter Ten

"I love sitting on your lap," I whisper to Ryan as I snuggle closer into him. I can smell his familiar scent. I run my hand over the back of his neck and through his hair over the back of his head.

"Please. Please Ryan. I beg you. Don't leave me. Don't ever leave me. I'll miss you too much. I'll be so alone without you," I whisper as tears start to trickle out of my eyes and wet my cheeks and slide down onto his neck.

He shifts slightly and looks at me as the tears drop on to him. I raise up and wipe my eyes with the back of my hand and lay my head back down onto his shoulder.

"Sorry. I'm sorry sweetie. I'm making you all wet," I say giggling.

When Ryan was in the hospital after his bicycle accident he was treated in the traumatic brain injury unit. A specialized multidisciplinary team took charge of his care. At one point, they asked me to see their psychologist who would counsel me about the possible residual effects of his injuries. I remember her so well. She was slim, middle aged and had her streaked blonde hair cut short in a kind of spiky, pixie style and except for a bright pink lipstick she wore almost no makeup.

"He may have some problems with impulse control in the future," she'd said quietly.

Impulse control? Is she warning me? Will he be violent now? My sweet, gentle Ryan?

"Violent? Do you mean that he could become violent with me? Is that what you're saying?" I'd blurted out my body starting to tremble.

I was sitting down in a hard backed chair in her office and I can remember sliding over to the side, almost falling off of the chair. She jumped up to assist me. But, I was able to straighten up and restore my position on my own. After that I had to keep my feet flat on the floor to stabilize myself during the rest of our meeting, because I was terrified of collapsing right in front of her.

"I'm sorry I know this is difficult," she'd said looking at me cautiously, as if to measure my reaction to what was coming next. "It's possible. Yes. But, what I meant is that certainly, most likely, he'll be more unpredictable. He must be a very logical kind of thinker to be as well positioned as he is in the legal community. But you need to prepare yourself that he may no longer make rational choices and decisions. This accident could have consequences for your future that you are not anticipating."

Her words are echoing in my brain. I'd had no idea then what she could possibly mean. How our future together could become so terribly changed.

"He may have poor impulse control and possibly give in to his impulses and make bad decisions. Not necessarily strike out at you, but he may become more impulsive in his actions and not be able to think through what the consequences might be," she continued, seeming to choose her words carefully. "Of course we don't know yet how he will be long term. We have to follow him and assess as we go."

Assess as we go! Those were her exact words. They are seared on to my brain. I'll never forget them! And now!

My left hip and thigh start to throb. My body isn't as strong as it was before all of this started. The anxiety and the depression have taken a toll on me physically as well as emotionally. And I'm not as active as before. I go to work. I come home. Before all of this, we were very busy as a couple. We went to dinner, to the movies, to concerts and to the theatre. But no more. And we walked. After dinner at home, we almost always took a walk. And if we dined out we'd pick a local spot so we could walk back and forth. Now it's as if I'm stuck in one place. And I'm aging fast. I have to start moving again and healing myself or I'm going to wither up and die alone in the damn condo.

Ryan feels warm and sturdy. Comforting and strong. I nestle in tighter against him and run my hand over his shirt front. I can smell the familiar scent of his citrusy aftershave lotion and the freshly laundered shirt. I need to get what little love I can from him because he'll be gone soon! Out of my life forever.

Something that I've never told anyone is that I was scared to marry him. When he asked me I hesitated. He had to persuade me. Reassure me. I guess I just had too many people that I was close to die on me. So I was terrified! Did I know then that it would end badly and well before it should?

My feet dangle over the arms of the large upholstered chair. His eyes are closed and his breathing blends in with mine, so it seems like it is just one person breathing. This is heaven. Just the two of us. Together always. Like before. A shot of anxiety spikes through me.

"I need you. I need someone in my life who is mine, only for me. And it has to be someone that I can look up to. Someone for me to love. To hold on to. I can't bear losing you. You've always been my one and only true love," I whisper hugging him around his neck as tightly as I can. "It feels so good to be close to you like this," I murmur as I kiss his temple and run my hand through his hair.

A huge sigh that ends in a moan escapes from somewhere very deep inside of me. And Ryan shifts to look at me, saying nothing. I know that I have to mentally brace myself for what I fear is coming. Because he is going to leave me! He might be silent. But, he's made that clear to me by his behaviour. And it's going to happen soon! No matter what I do, he won't stay with me. I can't stop him from going away. I can't prevent the inevitable! What has been set in motion will continue as if it has a life of its own. And I cannot control it.

CONSTANCE LECHMAN

Chapter Eleven

"Brooke!" Kylie says opening the door looking surprised.

"Am I wrong? Did I get the time wrong?" I reply to her looking at my watch.

"No, no of course not. Come on in. Go and make yourself comfortable and I'll make some coffee."

Usually Kylie is so organized that coffee would be ready and waiting. She looks like she just got up. She must have been napping. She really is tired out.

"Is everything OK Brooke?" Kylie asks as she follows me into the living room.

"It was gut wrenching," I say to Kylie, wiping my eyes with a tissue. "Just so damn get wrenching!" I say, turning to look at her as I plop down on her sofa.

My voice sounds shrill, almost unrecognizable. But I know that it's me, my voice. I lean back against the back of the sofa and blow my nose.

Instead of meeting in a café Kylie invited me to her home for coffee. She lives in a new build townhouse that is elegantly furnished in soft, muted tones of beige and cream that exude a soft, warm, comfortable ambience.

Kylie knows that I'm having more and more trouble holding in my feelings. So that's probably why she suggested her home. A wise move! Neither of us want me to lose it in a public place.

She's also aware that I have started seeing Lou Grimes. So far, I haven't told her anything about the therapy. I'm not the type of person to confide my feelings about anything so personal to someone other than Ryan. But I no longer have him for that outlet. And I'm feeling desperate to talk to someone. My chest aches unbearably from holding everything inside. I need to talk to her to tell her how I feel about Lou and the therapy.

"I know that I have to do this, but I didn't know that it would or could be this damn hard. It's excruciating!" I say as more tears trickle down my face and I take a deep breath. "I have new respect for all of my patients. It takes guts to really delve into yourself. To leap into all of the shit that you've spent a lifetime covering up, and burying so deep inside of yourself that you don't even remember or know that it's there."

I smack my knee with one hand and blow my nose with the ball of tissues I have in the other hand.

"I'm so sorry that you have to go through this Brooke. I always envied you and Ryan. Everyone has. You two have been the epitome of the perfect couple. The couple so in love that everyone could see it. No one would ever think that this could happen to the two of you," she says reaching across to take hold of my hand.

I stare at her. Perfect? We are or were perfect? Everyone thought that? It just goes to show that no one can always know what's really going on with someone else, or with another couple. Or for that matter really know what others think of you. You can look at them from the outside, but not see the inside and into their thoughts.

I feel my stomach start to clench, Things aren't perfect now. I take a deep breath and shake my head as I settle back into the corner of the cream coloured sofa that matches the upholstered arm chair in which Kylie is seated beside me.

"Do you feel like a failure Brooke?" Kylie says staring at me with a puzzled look on her face.

I stare at her. A failure? Why the hell would she ask me that?

"No!" I sputter and my voice squeaks as I say it. "No. Of course not! Why should I feel like a failure?"

"No. You're right. Sorry. Of course not. It didn't come out right. I. Uh I was just wondering how you were feeling. That's all," she says rubbing her eyes and yawning.

She looks very tired and the dark circles under her eyes seem even darker today. For the first time that I can remember she's not wearing any makeup at all and she is wearing the same pair of baggy jeans that I saw on her the last time we met with a short sleeved white T-shirt that is very rumpled and almost dingy looking. Strange! That's not like Kylie. She must be feeling really burned out from working on the novel.

"I just keep reviewing our life together," I say. "You know the memories and they're all good. I remember soon after we met, he, he said to me, he told me that he now recognized that he needed someone. He only realized that after meeting me. You know?" I say in a shaky voice as I brush more tears away from my cheeks.

Kylie nods. She stands up and walks the two short steps it takes to sit down next to me and pulls me into her arms and hugs me tightly.

A geyser spouts the sorrow out of me in great big sobs that won't stop. She holds me until I feel the pressure abate inside of me. I slowly pull away and wipe my eyes. I half smile at her.

"Thank you. Kylie you're a great friend. Thanks for listening," I say and then take a deep breath.

"Hey Brooke. No problem," she says getting up and returning to her chair. "You've always been there for me and for all of our friends. It's the least that I can do for you," she says and folds her legs under her in the chair in a sort of lotus position.

"Oh Kylie it's so sad. Because, now I know that it's true. He really is going to abandon me. But, the worst part is that even if he's going to leave me, I know that I can't let him go. Not yet," I blurt as I blow my nose.

Kylie nods and reaches over and pats my am. Slowly she unwinds herself and stands up and motions to me. I stand also and she pulls me back into a tight embrace and rubs my shoulders and back. I start to sob uncontrollably.

CONSTANCE LECHMAN

Chapter Twelve

"Where should I start?" I ask Lou Grimes.

I'm rapidly blinking my eyes in an effort to maintain control over any tears that might threaten to come. I'm so determined not to cry that I didn't take the precaution of folding a bunch of tissues into my hand. That took a lot of willpower! I've decided that I'm going to meet this head on. No more tears. I must remember that I will observe myself. I won't allow any feelings. I won't experience what I am saying. I will detach! I will watch and process as an observer of myself. I will not experience and drown in my feelings.

"Have you noticed that you asked me where you should start? Aren't you the one who made this appointment? Or did someone else make it for you?" he says speaking slowly in a very even tone as if he has all the time in the world.

He does have all the time to wait for me to experience the terrible pain inside of me. I grimace and then take a deep breath. He's right. I came to him. He didn't call me in. I'm not ten years old. This isn't the principal's office.

"Are you here on your own free will?" he asks, shifting slightly in his chair. "Or did someone tell you to come here today?" he says looking me squarely in the eyes.

I feel the familiar clenching ramp up in my stomach. He knows that I'm resisting. And I know it too. I don't want to open myself up to him or to anyone else ever again. I opened myself up to Ryan and now he's going, abandoning me. He's right. I know that I have to open myself up to him if I want to be able to master this mess. I have to go through hell if I'm going to get through this. Otherwise I need to get up and leave right now. I should just get the hell out of here fast. I uncross my knees and shift forward in my seat.

"OK," I say and swallow hard. "I'm not sleeping. I can't get to sleep because I can't stop my brain. It's on overdrive. Thinking and thinking and never stopping. So I can't rest. And I can't eat. I have no appetite. I have no desire to eat. I have to force myself to eat something, but I've lost weight. And I'm on edge. I'm practically jumping out of my skin and I'm irritable as hell. So I know. I mean, I can diagnose myself. I know that I'm depressed. But, I can't get rid of these dark thoughts. I just can't," I say in a rush as tears start to trickle out of the corners of my eyes and roll down my cheeks.

Damn it! I promised myself that I wouldn't cry.

"You say, dark thoughts."

I nod and blink back tears.

"How are you feeling right now with me?"

"Sad. Very, very sad." I sigh and blot my face. My eyes are sore from crying and my cheeks are damp.

"How are you experiencing this sadness, right now?"

A jolt of electricity rushes through me. He's pushing and he won't stop pushing me until I experience my feelings! I move back in the chair. My whole body has tensed. I brace my feet against the floor and press my shoulders against the back of the chair.

"Would you like to share with me how you experience this sadness with me?"

"Yeah. Umm, I ," I murmur. I look at him and blink. "I feel like I want to die. I'm losing everything. My whole life."

"That is not a feeling. That's a sentence. You haven't told me how you are experiencing this sad feeling."

He won't stop now. He's forcing me to break my own rules. I don't want to, because then I'll feel the pain. And it will simply be too much for me. No way. I can't do it!

Chapter Thirteen

"It's the hardest thing that I've ever done in my entire life," I say to Melinda. "Now I know what it's like to be on the other end of the therapy process," I say taking a deep breath. "Despite the anguish and the fact that I'd like to quit, I'm phoning because I do want to thank you for the referral. I really appreciate it. I know that he has a waiting list an arm long and that he took me out of professional courtesy. So thank you!"

When our call ends I stare at my cell and then put it down on the coffee table. I'm sitting in my living room. I'm numb. My mind is blank. I spot the remote control and pick it up and click on my favourite cooking channel. I lay back on the sofa and plump one of the toss cushions and rest it under my head and close my eyes. Bobby Flay is grilling. Didn't I hear that he left his wife? I must be wrong. He seems too nice to do that. Not all men are cheaters.

The phone rings and I jerk up and grab for it.

"Hello," I say quickly without looking at the screen.

"Hi Brooke. I'm just checking to see how your session went with Dr. Grimes."

"Hi Kylie, I'm. Uh I think it will help. Eventually. You know. I hope so. Because. Because it's not easy. You said something about opening up your heart in order to write a new life story. And I guess that's what I did when I met Ryan, He's such a loving, sweet man that he defrosted me. You know, you can only really see yourself in the way that you react in relationship with others. And. Well," I say sighing and rubbing my eyes. "I became a much softer, more loving person as our relationship evolved and now. Now I know that I'm going backwards. I'm freezing up again," I say as my voice cracks and tears start to flow.

I wipe them away with the sleeve of my T-shirt.

"I hate that you're going through this Brooke. You don't deserve this. Of all the people that I know, you really don't."

"I don't want to keep crying, but I can't seem to stop when I talk to you. I guess it's because I know that you care. I'm sorry for crying all the time."

"Please, feel free to talk, or cry, whatever you need to do. I'm your friend. Talk, cry, it doesn't matter. I'm here for you, you know that," she says softly.

She sounds like the old Kylie. My good friend Kylie. I sigh. I'm so glad that she's back to her old self. I need a friend right now. I need someone that I can rely on. I'm exhausted. I need a soft place where I can go. Where I don't have to face any conflict. I'm glad that whatever was bothering her or tiring her out is gone. I should ask her about it, but I can't. I just don't have the energy to ask her.

"When I first met him. He said to me, and I can remember it so clearly. He said, "I'm just a boy who grew up to be a man and I want to live my life fully and I want someone in my life who I can love totally," I say, taking the ball of tissues that I'm squeezing in my fist to dab at my eyes. "And I know, I know that you are that woman for me," he said.

I blink and look up at the ceiling and shake my head.

"That's beautiful Brooke. And you know that he meant it then. And, well it's still true. You both had each other for a long time. You have to hold on to those good memories of him and you together. That's what will get you through all of this misery. You know that, I don't have to tell you," she whispers.

Chapter Fourteen

"How can I help you if you won't even try to look at your feelings here with me," I ask Deborah Jones. "Isn't that why you consulted me in the first place?" I say raising my voice slightly for emphasis.

We're about ten minutes into our session in my private office. I have an office in the hospital as well as a private one close by for psychotherapy cases. Clients are usually referred to me for therapy by their physicians or social workers. Deborah's family doctor referred her when she consulted him for her feelings of depression and suicidal thoughts.

I grimace inwardly at how I sound. Just like the mirror image of Lou Grimes. I straighten my shoulders and try to focus on what Deborah is saying to me. She is a new patient and this is our third session. She initially told me that she came for help with her marital problems. But, she has been resistant to focusing on her inner rage and guilt. And her grief! Grief at losing her husband!

She just found out about a month ago that he's been having an affair for months. Instead of being in touch with her feelings she uses a lot of rationalization and intellectualization to defend against her anger. Of course, I know that I have to push through those defences and get her to explore her underlying conflict.

Kill him! Kill him! Do it! Kill him! You can do it! The thoughts intrude into my mind and erase Deborah from my brain. My heart starts to thump against my chest. And I can feel my throat tightening up. I take a deep breath.

Lately, these thoughts have been more frequent. Waking me up and stopping me from falling asleep and in the past two two days they've been a constant intrusion keeping me awake all night and preoccupying my mind wherever I am and no matter where I go. I'm exhausted. It's like I'm a robot on automatic pilot walking through life in a kind of torturous, invisible bubble.

No. Damn it! I can't do it. And I can't allow myself to think about it anymore. This has to stop. And how would I kill him? I know that I could give him a drug cocktail. Of course I can do that. I'm a doctor. I can write out prescriptions. But how can I even consider doing that? But I am. I am considering it! I must be considering it if these thoughts are occupying me night and day! I shift in my chair. I have to stop it! I have to prevent these thoughts from continuing to intrude into my mind.

It's better to have loved and lost. Isn't that what everyone says? No! At this moment I wish I'd never met him.

"The nerve of that bastard! I could feel myself really getting enraged," Deborah says in a loud voice jolting my focus back to her.

"Could we focus on that rage and how you experienced it," I say to her.

I need to focus on her, not me. She came to me for help. She trusts me to help her. And I'm here because I do want to help her, despite my mental state, which is a complete and total mess. And hearing the anger in her voice means that we're getting closer to a breakthrough. For the first time she is actually talking about and experiencing her fury at her husband. Progress!

Deborah sought help after she walked in on him naked in bed with the other woman. Someone that he works with. And until now she's only cried. She's never even admitted to having any anger at him. This admission means the work that we've been doing is really starting to pay off. Finally!

I know that's what Lou Grimes wants to be able to do in order to help me. He's pushing and pressing me hard in order to try to penetrate my defences to get at my deepest feelings and all the conflict that is intertwined with them. All the rage and guilt and grief that I know intellectually must be there.

"I wanted to hit him," Deborah snaps. "I had a cup of take out coffee in my hand and, and I could actually picture what it would be like to throw it at him! It was surreal, as if I could see my arm throw it, like it was in slow motion!"

My mind starts to clear. I sit up straighter and I lock eyes with Deborah who looks angry.

"How did you experience that force of lashing out at him inside of you?" I say to her in a firm and confident voice.

CONSTANCE LECHMAN

Chapter Fifteen

"Have you noticed that you want to talk about your brother dying, but you never speak about his partner?" Lou Grimes says to me, levelling his gaze right through my eyes and into the depths of my mind.

"His partner?" I ask as my stomach starts to contract.

Partner? Who the hell is he talking about? He died young so he didn't have a wife. He never even had time to make a friend! I shift in the chair and the leather squeaks when I move so I stop moving. I'm rigid. My whole body has tensed as if I'm coiled up ready to spring. Spring out of here!

What the hell is he talking about? Suddenly a shock of electricity runs up and down my spine. My mouth opens and then closes. I stare at him.

"You. You mean my mother? Is that who you mean?" I look at him and he gazes back at me remaining silent.

My mother! My heart has revved up and it is racing.

"My mother did her best, like any mother would. She had a lot to contend with, first my brother dying. Then my father!" I say barely audible.

I'm aware that my voice has become raspy and weak. It sounds thin. Is it possible for a voice to be thin? I can feel the tension increasing in my back and shoulders. He's hit a nerve because my body is reacting and I don't know how to respond. My mind is a whirl of thoughts. My feet start to shift. Run! Go now. You don't have to do this. Go! Get out of here. I grasp the arms of the chair and take a deep breath.

"I have a recurring dream. In the dream I have a sister and she grabs my hair and she yanks it. And it comes right out. And I see her holding my hair in her hand. Like a scalp! I'm terrified! At first she looks at me surprised. Then my mother appears and starts to laugh and then my sister laughs. And then I always wake up!"

I'm aware that my underarms are wet and there's perspiration on my upper lip. My heart is thundering in my chest. I can barely breathe! I swallow to try to get rid of the blockage in my throat. I need to get some air!

"Do you have a sister?" he asks, raising his left eyebrow.

He knows that I don't. I've told him about my brother.

"No, as I told you. Only a brother who died," I snap.

Lou studies me for a couple of moments. I stare back at him holding my breath.

"Could we look at your dream?" he says slowly and firmly. "You say that in your dream your sister pulls your hair out. She scalps you and your mother laughs. And then your sister laughs too."

"Oh my God!" My hand flies to my mouth covering it and tears start to flow from my eyes. "My mother! She laughs first and then my sister. She only laughs after. After my mother laughs. My mother is the one who laughs!" I say in a hoarse whisper.

I'm aware that my hands have started to shake. They've joined my heart in moving entirely on their own. My body is out of my control! He's right! It was my mother who was attacking me. She should have protected me! Not laugh at me!

"So in your dream, your sister was your mother's agent, her partner in tormenting you. But, your mother was the leader, wasn't she?" Lou asks quietly.

I nod at him. I can feel my feet digging into the floor beneath me. My calves are aching. I lift one foot, then the other and unclench my toes that are curled inside of my shoes.

"I've never thought of it in that way before. But, yes. She should have intervened. Children quarrel. They need an adult, a parent, a mother to intervene, to be a referee. A fair and neutral intermediary. Instead my mother was being mean to me by hiding behind my sister in the dream. And encouraging her by laughing. She was the main one. And all this time I've focused on my brother dying. But my mother died too when he did! Apparently, she was never the same after my brother died. My aunt told me that she never got over it. She became a depressed and bitter woman. I guess that's what I ended up with afterwards. A mother who was never there for me again."

I realize that my heart is still pounding and my hands are starting to shake so badly that I squeeze my palms together to steady them. My brain feels like it's going to explode. I want to lay down and curl up into a tiny ball, right here, right in front of Dr. Lou Grimes! Instead. I force my shoulders back and sit as straight as I can and I nod at Lou. Tears trickle down my cheeks.

"She robbed me of us, me and her. She was never happy. I grew up fighting with her and she died young. She was only forty five! She got cancer, breast cancer actually and she gave up really. She never tried to live after that. It was terrible. I lost her too! Twice! First, when my brother died. And then because of the damn cancer."

"So she died off in your life a long time ago," he says softly. "You must have a lot of mixed feelings about that. Don't you?"

How pathetic! She died! My father was already gone! And my brother too! My twin. My mirror image. All dead! No wonder Ryan has been so important to me. There's nothing I wouldn't do for Ryan. He was my saviour! My rock. And now! He's left me alone too!

I nod at him as I start to sob. The tears are blurring his image. But, I'm actually seeing more clearly. And along with the grief that's pouring out of me I'm feeling the intensity of the force of volcanic rage that I have towards all of them inside of me! Every damn bloody one of them!

CONSTANCE LECHMAN

Chapter Sixteen

"I think it's starting to help me feel a little calmer so that's good," I say to Kylie.

We're standing next to each other in the reception area of a local Greek taverna that has a great bar and serves generous amounts of delicious food. They're known for their grilled sea bass and octopus ceviche.

We're waiting to be seated with the rest of our friend's circle. We entered almost at the same moment and have only been waiting about two minutes. But other than a hello and how are you, Kylie has been very quiet. She seems lost deep in thought as if she's in another world.

"So thanks. Thanks for all of your support," I say smiling at her. "It means a lot to me Kylie."

She looks at me as if she's seeing me for the first time.

"No problem Brooke. Any time. Now if I could just fix my own problems then we'll both be on the right track," she says sarcastically and then snorts and shakes her head as she starts to trail the hostess who has arrived and indicated to us to follow her to our table.

I stand paralyzed for a moment and then I quickly walk behind both of them. I'm feeling numb. Problems? Kylie has problems? No wonder she seems so distracted. I've been so full of my own misery that I haven't even noticed that Kylie needs support too. I've been incredibly selfish. I feel my cheeks burning. I need to do better. I've lost everyone else. I don't want to lose my friends too. Especially Kylie. We go back such a long way. Her and Billy. We've always connected well as two couples, and had lots of good times as a foursome.

As I arrive at the empty chair next to where Kylie is starting to seat herself I look in her direction.

She's smiling at Georgia and Karen who arrived earlier and have already ordered and are sipping glasses of white wine. There are two large platters of mixed hors d'oeuvres in the middle of the table and a stack of small plates and a pile of white napkins for each of us to serve ourselves.

Kylie's hurting and obviously she didn't want to burden me with her problems. Do our other friends know what's wrong with her? Was she able to confide in them? Is it just me that's out of the loop? And what do they know about my issue? I've said very little to anyone except Kylie, Melinda, and of course Lou Grimes. Naturally, people know when your living situation changes with your husband. It's a total no brainer. They get the picture very quickly and no one wants to ask a lot of questions and be seen as nosy. Besides they know that I only say what I want others to know. I've never been big on talking about any kind of personal issues. Instead, I've been the one that other people tell their deepest, darkest and most personal secrets to without any hesitation.

The handsome, young waiter makes his way over to us and puts a paper coaster down in front of me and then Kylie, and smiles at us.

"A glass of the chardonnay please," I say pointing to my selection on the wine menu and smiling back at him.

Kylie turns to the waiter to give him her order. I need to try to talk to her, but this isn't the right time or the right place.

"This is a good break," I say as the waiter reappears and places my wine down and then puts Kylie's order of her favourite merlot on her coaster. "Look I'm sorry. I know that I've been very wrapped up in my problems and I've, I mean I haven't even asked you how you're doing. I'm sorry to hear that you have been having a problem. Can I help?"

"Don't worry about it Brooke. Here, do you want something to eat," she says handing me a small plate from the stack next to her, as she nods towards the platter of flaky spanakopita, tzatziki, large green olives, slices of feta and toasted pita triangles.

Our eyes meet as I shake my head. She looks incredibly sad. Very tired and very sad. How could I have not seen that before now? What on earth is wrong with me? I'll call her tomorrow. I will make this up to her. I have to!

Chapter Seventeen

"I can't believe how selfish I am," I say to Lou Grimes the next morning. "I'm realizing that I'm not the kind of friend that I thought I was. My dear friend Kylie is having problems and I didn't even know about it! She didn't share it with me. She obviously felt that I wasn't there for her. I've been very, very selfish!"

"Kylie?" He asks with a frown.

"Yes! My best friend Kylie. She's going through some personal problems and I didn't even suspect that something was wrong. Of course I noticed that she seemed tired. But everyone else seems to be in the know. And me, well I've been so wrapped up in my own problems that I never even noticed what she was going through," I reply sharply.

I shake my head and sigh.

"But do you notice how you want to talk about Kylie and her problems and you use these sentences about friendship and selfishness. But, as usual you don't say how you feel deep inside. And you are avoiding to talk about your mother. Do you see that?" He asks, his forehead creasing even deeper.

I sit back in my chair and stare at him. Damn it! What the hell does he want from me? I feel terrible about not being there for Kylie. Is he saying that I treat women badly because of my mother? What the hell does he want from me? Blood? I can feel my pulse racing and I turn my head and look at the tree branches outside of his window.

"Do you see what I mean?" he repeats and settles deeper into his chair.

I can feel my cheeks heating up and my heart pounding.

"Why do you always attack me? Why am I never not good enough for you?" I snap.

"How do you feel towards me right now?" he says staring at me, his feet firmly planted on the floor.

"Fine," I mutter looking down at my hands. I curl my fingers and tightly squeeze both of my fists.

"Fine is a word. It's not a feeling. And look at your clenched fists."

"OK. I'm pissed. OK! Are you happy?" I can feel an explosion moving through my core right up to my chest.

"Right now," he persists.

"Angry! I'm angry, I'm angry at you. I'm angry at Ryan. At my mother. Everyone lets me down! I'm bursting with anger! I want to explode!" I say smacking my knee.

"Can you describe that explosion, that anger, that rage that you have inside of you right now?

"It's like a bomb going off inside," I snap.

"Do you feel like lashing out?" he quickly asks.

"Yes. Yes." I say aware of my fists still tightly clenched in my lap. I look at them. I nod at Lou. "Yes! I could kill her right now! And him too! And Ryan, he let me down too!" I say as my body jerks.

"But do you notice that at first rather than talk about your rage to me you preferred to tell me sentences. And you didn't want to describe the experience. Instead you smack your knee. You didn't want to say how you really feel about lashing out. To kill! You said that it's the same with Ryan and with your mother! You have intellectualized your rage and internalized it and you feel depressed and instead of killing them, you can't breathe. You are killing yourself! Isn't that what you are doing? You rationalize it and bury it. As deeply as possible. Isn't that what you have done for your entire life?" he says pressing his point by speaking slowly and emphasizing each word making it impossible for me to avoid what he is saying to me.

I look at him and I nod my head slowly. I look at my hands that are now lying open and relaxed in my lap.

"I had no idea of how angry I still am at my mother! And at Ryan too! I had no idea," I say looking Lou in the eyes and shaking my head.

"Ryan! Never. I never even knew that I was so angry at him!"

I feel my hands start to tremble.

Chapter Eighteen

"Hi Kylie," I say as I readjust the phone in my hand.

I'm laying on my sofa with my head and shoulders propped up on a cushion with a throw over my legs. It's 8:30 in the evening and I'm tired after a day at work and my session afterwards with

Lou. I want to apologize to Kylie for not being there for her and if she feels like she wants to talk I want her to know that I'm here for her.

"How are you and Billy?" I ask her easing into the conversation.

"You mean William!" Kylie snarls.

My neck jerks and I hold the phone in front of my face and stare at it before speaking.

"William? William is Billy?" I stammer.

I never knew he was actually a Willam. Neither Kylie nor Billy ever used the name Willam before. I guess it's obvious, but he's always been Billy.

"Yeah. William. Mr William Alexander," Kylie hisses.

"Is there something wrong with Billy, I mean William. I mean you sound really angry. I didn't know his name was William. I guess it's obvious. I mean I should have known. It's completely obvious of course. But he's always been Billy, you know."

I know that I'm rambling. Kylie's obvious rage has rattled me. My mind is blank.

"I'm done with Mr. William Alexander, that shitty bastard!" she spits into the phone.

William? Bastard! Billy is William? And shitty? And a bastard! What the hell has happened?

"What? What happened Kylie?" I ask in a squeaky voice.

Silence. Then I hear her sniff a few times.

"Kylie? What happened with you and Billy?" I'm gripping the phone so tightly that my fingers are hurting. I try to flex them in order to relax my grip and ease the aching.

"What do you think? The usual," she snaps in a loud voice. "He met some young skank who he's been obviously boinking for weeks. Who knows maybe for months!"

Billy? I'm numb. This can't be happening. My mind is paralyzed! I'm completely stripped of all thoughts. I picture Billy laughing, looking at Kylie and hugging her. Billy is a big teddy bear kind of a guy. A real sweetheart. Everyone loves Billy. No not Billy too! Why does this happen? Is it some middle age fling, a phase that men and women, especially men, have to go through in a marriage? This is nuts!

"I'm so, so sorry Kylie. I didn't know. I, I'm shocked! I had no idea that you guys were having a problem in your relationship. I'm really sorry! When did all of this happen?"

Oh no! She already said weeks, maybe months. Oh my God!

"I mean when did you find out about all of this?"

I can feel my heart racing. Am I really hearing right?

"I'm so angry. I could kill that asshole! And I just might!" she snarls.

I shudder. Kylie wants to kill Billy! How could this be happening? I know Billy loves Kylie and she's been crazy about him since the moment she laid eyes on him.

"But!" I blurt out.

"I don't know when it started," Kylie interjects. "Weeks, months? Who knows? Maybe even years! Is this just one of a series of tramps in his life? I don't know! But, I just found out and I didn't want to burden you. You had your own big problems with Ryan. I couldn't pile this shit on top of that crap."

"I'm sorry. I should have been more..."

"No. No. You've been so heartbroken, I couldn't add to it," Kylie interjects. "Me! I'm angry. I'm mad as hell. He's ruined everything. Our family, our home. Everything!" I hear her take a deep breath.

"How could he do this to our kids? Me, that's one thing! But our kids! They have always idolized him. He was their hero! Now he's nothing but a traitorous shithead! A completely disgusting piece of shit!" she shouts.

"What can I do to help?" I say wiping my wet palms on my jeans.

I yank the throw off and sit up on the edge of the sofa with my feet on the floor. I can feel the perspiration trickling down my temples. My heart is pounding in my chest. Thank God Ryan and I don't have children. That's one less heartache to have to deal with now.

"I want to kill him! Do me a favour. Brooke. And please do it for me! Kill the bastard for me!" Kylie shrieks into the phone. "And do it quick. In the meantime I'm going to kick his ass out of here tonight."

I hear the dial tone and I stare at the phone. What the hell? I can't believe what I just heard. Poor Kylie! This is terrible. I wish I could do something to help her. How could Billy do this? She's an amazing woman! I feel nauseated thinking about Kylie. What a terrible shock for her! No wonder she's been looking so drained. Anyone, no matter how strong or talented, would be bowled over by this.

Is it the sex? Is it always about sex when a guy has an affair? And then what? After the excitement of the new sexual encounter fades, then what?

Obviously, they're not thinking about the after part, the consequences, just the thrill of some exciting sex in the present moment. That's all that matters I guess.

What the hell Billy! How stupid can you be? And I thought you were different. Obviously, you're not! You are definitely not the man that I thought you were. Not at all!

Chapter Nineteen

"There's nothing better than love," I say to the tall man in the long, black coat.

He's wearing a wide brimmed hat and he's standing with his back to me. His dark hair is streaked with grey and it curls on to the back of his collar.

"When Ryan looks at me and his face shines I can feel his love for me," I say to the man. "It radiates out of him. He glows and I glow in return. I can actually feel what it's like to glow! There's nothing better than that in this whole world. That's what life is about. To feel love for someone who looks at you with love. Finding true love, that's what is most important. And! And, I know for certain that there's nothing that Ryan wouldn't do for me if I asked him. So you need to know that it's the same with me. I'll do anything for him. He just needs to ask me! He can count on me. Because I'll do whatever he wants me to do!" I say emphasizing each word.

The man slowly turns around to look at me and I gasp! His face is missing! There's only a pulpy, red and black hole where his face should be! My heart starts to pound.

I wake up perspiring. I rub my eyes and stare at the ceiling and take deep breaths. I turn over and look at the clock. It's 3:40 am! I turn on to my back and close my eyes and take deep, slow breaths.

"No Ryan! No! No! Please don't! Don't do this! No! Please don't!" I scream as he leans over me and closes his fingers around my throat.

I try to pull his hands off of me but he's too strong for me. I can't budge his hands off of my neck. He puts his knee on my waist and then presses down with his full weight. I try to wriggle free, but I can't move any part of my body because now he's pressing his entire body against me too tightly. I'm entombed by him!

"No! P...Please, no!" I gurgle at him.

But he keeps squeezing my neck until I can no longer breathe. I'm dying! I've stopped breathing!

I jerk awake. My heart is pounding out of my chest. I rub my hand in a circular motion over my heart to quell the pressure. I pull the covers up around my neck, shiver and hug myself. I close my eyes. Ryan had his hands around my neck! I could feel him exerting pressure and pushing his thumbs deep into my flesh until I could no longer breathe! I rub my hand over my eyes. Thank God I was only dreaming! I open my eyes wide as I run the nightmare around and around in my head.

I'm seeing Lou Grimes later today. I'll have ro choice. I'll have to tell him about the man with no face and worse, about the second nightmare I just had about Ryan strangling me. A tear runs out of the corner of my right eye and slowly edges down my cheek. Maybe it means something different. After all, as a psychiatrist I know that the manifest content and the underlying meaning of a dream are not always the same. Maybe Lou can help me make something else out of it. Something other than Ryan killing me!

A volt of electricity shoots through the length of my entire body. No! What am I thinking? I can't tell Lou! Who knows what he'll be able to make out of this nightmare! I don't want to go there! And the man with no face! My stomach flip-flops. And I shiver.

I pull the covers over my head and start to sob. Why? I slowly move the covers away and while I'm still laying on my back, I edge over to the side of the bed and slowly slide my legs over the edge and then mechanically put my feet down on to the area rug. I sit up and brush the tears away with both of my hands.

My nightmares keep intruding into my thoughts while I shower and dress and it seems to take me forever to get ready. Every time I remember what it felt like to have Ryan's hands on my neck, I start to tremble. I keep taking deep breaths, and push the thoughts out of my mind, but the horrible feeling of dread in the pit of my stomach won't disappear. Maybe repeating both of the nightmares to Lou will help to dissipate the anxiety. But I don't see him until six o'clock this evening. I take a big breath in and out to try to ease the pressure in my chest.

Thankfully I can walk to work. Maybe the cool, sunny morning and a brisk pace will help me to ease the heavy weight that I feel inside.

It's Tuesday and my day of the week to work in the outpatient clinic of our hospital's psychiatric department. Senior staff are responsible for each day of the clinic's operation. We're charged with seeing new patients, assessing them and prescribing a treatment plan. Part of the process also involves my teaching the psychiatric residents who are doing their rotation in the clinic.

Many of the patients that we see will be followed in the multidisciplinary programs that we have established in the department. A few will need to return to see me or one of the residents for monitoring of any medication that is prescribed. There is a network of general practitioners in the community and a multidisciplinary team of nurses, social workers and occupational therapists who work with me in the clinic to provide the follow up that's needed by the patients.

I'm known as a good diagnostician. I love the variety of new patients that we see each week and I take pride in making sure that each new case has a thorough treatment plan that includes interdisciplinary input and follow up. Resources are scarce but I make sure that we do the best we can for each patient that we assess.

Last week one of the new cases that we saw was a young woman who had witnessed a murder in her rooming house and was suffering from post-traumatic stress. Another patient was an elderly male who had a panic attack at the dentist. We were able to determine that his panic attack was linked to the one year anniversary death of his wife of fifty years. There was also a severely depressed and highly suicidal patient who we admitted to the psychiatric inpatient ward.

As well, we saw several cases with anxiety disorder and a young nineteen year old male who was socially isolated from his peers and told me that he thought people on the TV were talking directly to him. I diagnosed him as schizophrenic. Despite the fact that he'd been suffering for two years his family had avoided taking him to a doctor because they were afraid of psychiatrists. He required medication and close follow up of his progress by one of our residents. I'm available to the resident for consultation at any time. Our team social worker will also be providing the very perplexed patient and his frightened family with regular supportive counselling.

Thinking about the clinic and the patients we help has eased the pressure in my chest. Thank God for my work! I start to grab for my keys and cell phone from the hall console table. As I reach for them, the phone starts to ring. I look at the screen. Oh my God! It's Billy! Or is it William? Another nightmare! My heart starts to thump.

CONSTANCE LECHMAN

Chapter Twenty

"Hello Billy," I say in as even a tone of voice as I can manage.

I'm shocked and I don't want him to know how surprised I am. In all of the years that I've known Kylie and Billy I don't think that he has ever phoned me!

"Brooke. Hi. How are you doing?"

"Uh, I. I'm surprised to hear from you," I say mentally kicking myself.

"Look I need your help. It's Kylie. She's gone crazy!" he says talking quickly.

"Crazy? What? What do you mean, crazy?" I say pulling the phone away from my ear to look at it.

Aren't I the only one who is going crazy? Isn't it me? What's he talking about? He's the problem. Isn't he?

"She's accusing me of having an affair. Multiple affairs in fact. Multiple! Good God Brooke! She's totally irrational. I can't even talk to her without her going off of the deep end. Screaming and ranting and pacing. She's out of control," he says sounding breathless as he stops speaking.

"Well, are you telling me that you aren't having an affair or that you didn't have one?" I ask him.

"Brooke you know me. You've known me almost as long as you've known Kylie and even longer than you've known Ryan. And I know that I'm no Ryan in your eyes. I know that. I am NOT. Sorry, I'm sorry for shouting. But, I'm not having an affair," he says emphasizing the word affair. "I've never cheated on Kylie. Never. I love her. You need to believe me. Look, all I'm asking," he says and pauses, breathing heavily into the phone. "The reason I called you is that Kylie needs help. You're her best friend, she might listen to you. I can't get through to her. God knows that I've tried," he says, his voice cracking.

Billy's right. I have known him about the same length of time as Kylie and longer than my husband. I picture myself with Kylie and Billy at university, the three of us, with a mix of other students, drinking mugs of draft beers together at the local pub. Billy and Kylie met as grad students and married after they both started their professional careers. So in fact I've been friends with him a long time. He's been like a brother to me. And Billy sounds sincere. What the hell is going on? Is Kylie wrong about him? Or is he trying to triangulate me to get me aligned with him against Kylie? Why? What's in it for him to do that?

"Look Billy. You're absolutely right about us being friends for a long time. I'm incredibly upset about all of this. And you need to know, and this is important. You need to know that I do not want to get between you and Kylie. Nor do I want to side with one of you against the other," I say firmly. "Neutral. I want to be completely neutral in this," I emphasize.

"I get it Brooke," Billy interjects before I can say any more. "I understand. Really! I only want you to help her. She needs help, Brooke. And I can't get through to her. Someone needs to help her. If you won't, then what am I supposed to do? She refuses to go and see anyone to get help for herself."

"What about suggesting that you both go to marriage counselling? Tell her that you'll go with her to see a professional, someone completely objective, a neutral person," I say looking at my watch. "You both need help to work this out before it gets any worse."

"I did suggest that to her and she just went crazy screaming at me. Wild! Telling me it was my problem. That she couldn't take it anymore. I don't even know what she's talking about! Would you suggest it to her Brooke? Because I'll go. I'll go to anyone you say. I'll do anything. I promise," he says sounding deflated as his voice trails off.

"Hang on a minute Billy. I'm trying to get out the door. Just wait a sec," I say as I pull my coat off of the hanger in the coat closet and pull it on switching the phone from hand to hand.

I close and lock the door and step outside onto the sidewalk. I take in a deep breath of the cool, fresh morning air.

"You know Billy that I can't promise anything. She's very angry. But, I'll call Kylie this morning and see where she's at," I say as I start striding quickly to the hospital. "I'm going to recommend to her that the two of you talk either with or without someone. Frankly, I think you need expert help, but whatever, you need to sit down and work this out together. Please, for the sake of your marriage! I'm sorry, but I've gotta go or I'll be late for the start of the clinic," I say ending the call.

My heart is beating quickly and it's not the fast walking pace that's doing it. My mind is awhirl with

Kylie and Billy. I can't believe what's happening! I love both of them. They've both been very good friends. And I'm loyal to both of them. But who is telling me the truth? Kylie? Why would she say that Billy is having affairs? And Billy? He's always been a straight shooter. And what is the truth? I feel a deep throbbing at my left temple. I reach for the zipper on my hand bag and rummage inside for the bottle of Tylenol.

Chapter Twenty-One

"So would you like to tell me how I can be of help to you?" I say to the new client who is sitting across from me.

I am seeing Mark, a young university student, on a pro bono basis in my private office, for the first time. He was referred by my colleague Gary

Ryerson for further assessment and psychotherapy after he was seen at a community health clinic by Gary as part of his volunteer outreach.

Gary and I trained together and we know each other's professional strengths. He felt that Mark needed immediate help and that he was a good candidate for psychotherapy, but he was leaving for an out of town conference in the next week. He pleaded with me to take him on as a client in my private practice because he knows that I have expertise in grief therapy.

Gary's exact words to me were, "you'll see, he's an intelligent, serious and articulate young man who is also very psychologically minded. This guy appears to have very good coping skills and is in a crisis situation due to the sudden death of a single parent. I think he's an excellent candidate for dynamic crisis intervention. I don't want him to get the wrong kind of therapeutic help. He needs what you can do for him Brooke."

Mark's a handsome, well groomed young man with a very sad face. He's neatly dressed in a light sage green denim shirt, chocolate brown cords and black sports shoes.

"Dr. Ryerson referred me to you. My mother died about three months ago and I'm, well I'm having trouble studying," he says as tears trickle out of the corners of both eyes. "So I went to the clinic to get some help. I don't want to fail my year," he mumbles as the tears increase.

"Three months ago?" I say softly as I feel a mixture of sadness and sympathy welling up inside of me.

He nods and shifts his body pressing himself against the back of the chair. His hands are gripping the chair's arms.

"Yes. It sounds strange to even say it, It's like it happened a minute ago and at the same time it's like she was never here. That's strange isn't it?" he says looking at me, as if he's pleading with me.

"What happened to your mother," I ask purposely using the word mother to push the realization of the importance of her death.

"She, she had cancer and it was so quick. We thought that she was going to be OK. But she wasn't. She didn't even make it all the way through her chemo treatment. Apparently she was terminal when they diagnosed her. But she didn't, she didn't tell me that part. I didn't know," he sputters, slapping the arm of the chair and looking up at the ceiling.

He wipes the tears from his face with the back of his hand. I can feel my eyes starting to water. This young man is in terrible pain and my reaction is an automatic reflex in me. I can't stop my own tears from forming.

This is obviously an acute crisis situation. He needs to deal with his grief. So it's my job to push him to explore the anguish and to do a review of his life with his mother because he will need to experience the pain if he is going to be able to successfully move forward in his life. Because he's right. Otherwise he will fail his courses and then he may end up stuck and in a permanent rut.

The positive thing about a crisis in an otherwise well functioning person is that the person has access to the deepest unconscious conflicts in their psyche, because it is in a state of flux, and in that way it can become a growth promoting point in their life if it's handled properly in therapy. On the other hand, if it's not dealt with skillfully, it can become a chronic and crippling psychological situation. Many therapists who are not well trained are unable to assess the patient's strengths correctly and do not know how to intervene in order to do this kind of work. Instead they give reassurance and supportive talk, while the deepest layer of feelings gets buried and is not dealt with in order to free the patient and enhance their emotional well being.

"Would you like to tell me more about your mother?" I say as I begin to feel my chest starting to compress.

I take a deep breath. I can't let him down. I want to do my best for him. He's relying on me for that!

He looks at me and hesitates.

"When did you find out about her cancer? When was that? Where were you when she told you?"

"I'd just come home from school," he says and stops and takes a deep breath and wipes his eyes.

"What room were you in when she told you?" I want to put him in that exact moment by picturing the scene.

"In the kitchen. We were standing in the kitchen. I knew that she had an appointment with the doctor that day. And I could see that she had been crying. I was surprised. I mean. I wasn't expecting it. So I asked her what was wrong. And," he says and stops and takes a deep breath. "And I never told her before she died that I loved her. I should have. I should have told her," he says between deep sobs.

Mark is suffering with a painful mixture of guilt and grief that is typical of mourning. This is a normal reaction to losing his mother. It's also a major crisis in his life and he needs therapeutic help to work his way through this. This is clear cut for me, but today I'm struggling. I feel my chest tightening up as if a weight is pushing down on it. My voice is raspy. It feels weak, like there's no power inside of me to get the words out. But I have to do my job. I can't stop. I can't let him down. And I won't!

"You said that you were in the kitchen? What was the conversation between the two of you?" I ask knowing that I am pressing him to relive the moment.

As I'm pushing him to re-experience the feelings with his mother and to relive the pain, I suddenly remember my father's funeral. It was a bright sunny day and I remember riding in the big, black car. That's my only memory of his funeral. And truthfully I don't know if it's even a real memory or something that my mind has made up. Everything else about that day is blocked out!

"In. Uh..Yeah. We were in the kitchen and," he starts to sob again with his face bent down holding it in his hands.

I wait a few moments before speaking. I take a few deep breaths.

"You said that you were in the kitchen," I say pushing the thought of my father away and taking another deep breath.

He nods at me and wipes his eyes.

"She told me she had cancer about two months before she died," he says tapping his fist against his heart as rivers of tears are streaming down his face. "It hurts," he moans.

He stops speaking and examines his hands, and takes a deep breath before reaching for a tissue on the table between us to blow his nose. He pulls out several emptying the box.

"My Dad left us when I was a baby and it was always the two of us. I have a girlfriend. We've been together for about a year. But, I still lived with my Mom, because I was going to school. I work part-time and I was saving up my money to get my own place after I graduated."

"So it was just the two of you always together, and now suddenly she's gone," I say at the same moment that a sharp pain whips through my chest.

I lean forward in my chair to ease the vice like grip that's encircling my upper body. I shift in my seat and take some more deep breaths.

Mark nods at me and starts to sob and rock slightly in his chair.

I feel a tear trickle down my face. He's crying so hard that he'll never notice the tears in my eyes or that I'm gasping for air. I push my shoulders back and take several deep breaths to try to release the pressure inside of my chest. Focus. Focus on Mark. Not on my father. Not on anyone else. I need to do my best for Mark! I have a job to do! Do it!

I reach for another box of tissues that's sitting on my desk and hand it towards him. He grabs on to it and pulls several out and blows his nose and then reaches for another handful and wipes his eyes and sets the box down on the table.

"She did everything for me when I was growing up. She is..." he jerks in the chair and looks me in the eyes and shakes his head. "She was..." he whispers and his voice cracks. "...was really strong. She worked and she was always there for me. I could talk to her about anything," he says reaching for another bunch of tissues.

I take a deep breath and look at this young man with the tears streaming down his face who is in so much pain from such a terrible loss in his life. His mother, his best friend, his partner and really, his soul mate is gone! And it's all I can do to quell the surge of grief that bursts up inside of me and to prevent myself from sobbing.

Chapter Twenty-Two

"Hi Kylie," I mouth the words and wave at her.

She smiles and waves back. Kylie's about ten yards ahead of me on the sidewalk. She was eager to meet me when I called and suggested coffee at our favourite café. In fact, I was relieved that she sounded like the old Kylie, happy and carefree.

She stops and waits for me and we hug as we meet. I put my arm around her and squeeze her shoulder and smile at her as we walk up the steps of the café.

"I'm so glad that you called Brooke. What a great suggestion! You know how much I love the chocolate croissants here," she says to me as we pull out our chairs and sit down. "You wait here, I'll order for us. Your usual?" she says as she jumps up and starts toward the counter.

"Yes, thank you," I call out back to her.

I'm smiling, but my heart is beating quickly. She seems very different from the frantic woman that I spoke to the other day. It's as if it never happened. But it did. What's going on? It's like Jekyll and

Hyde. I've known her for years, but the thing that's been nagging at me is how in the past year or so she's been absent from my life. It was only when I started having a terrible problem with Ryan that she reached out to me and re-entered my life and we became closer again. She'd called me when she heard about Ryan and was very upset about him and very comforting and encouraging to me. I've been trying to go back in my mind to try to figure out when and why we got so distant from each other before that, but it's been eluding me.

And of course since I wasn't seeing Kylie very much I also had little or no contact with Billy. So whether or not he was straying, I couldn't tell because I've been so completely out of the picture.

I look around the cafe that is almost empty except for an elderly couple sitting across the room from us who appear to be deep in conversation and a young man who is wearing earphones sitting in the corner busily scrolling on his phone.

"I know what you want to talk to me about," Kylie says as she returns and sits down.

She's talking very quickly. And I watch as she rummages around in her purse. She stops and without retrieving anything puts her purse down on the floor still wide open.

"And I want you to know that I'm here for you. I know how hard it is for you right now with Ryan and everything. So don't hold back. It's OK," she gushes, smiling at me and reaching for my hand, she pats it.

I'm staring at her. My mind is blank.

Thankfully, the barista calls out that our coffee order is ready. Kylie leaps up and starts towards the counter, turns and comes back and retrieves her purse and goes to the counter and after fumbling with her purse and then her wallet she manages to pay by tapping with her credit card.

I watch her as she returns grinning, with a tray of cappuccino and a chocolate croissant for her and an espresso and a plain croissant for me. Her hands are shaking and the cutlery and cups on the tray rattle slightly as she sets it down on the table between us.

"Your order madam!" she says giggling and handing me some cutlery and a large paper napkin.

I notice that my hand is shaking slightly as I reach for my coffee and the small white plate with my croissant. The espresso cup clinks in the saucer as I set it down in front of me. Kylie removes her coffee and pastry and rests the tray on the floor against the legs of her chair.

"So how are you?" Kylie asks before taking a large bite of her croissant.

"Well, you know, nothing's changed with me and Ryan, but I think that I'm feeling better now that I'm seeing Dr. Grimes," I reply.

"That's great Brooke. He must be a very good therapist then," she says quickly, nodding her head at me.

"Yeah. I guess so. It was a good decision for me to get help. That's for sure. It's not easy, but it's a good thing. It feels good to have someone to share the burden with, you know, someone who can be objective," I say and hesitate. "What about you Kylie. Do you think it would be useful for you and Billy to see a marital therapist?"

Kylie jumps up so suddenly that the tray clatters down to the floor. My whole body jerks and I spill my coffee on the table as I put the cup down. The elderly couple are staring at us.

"Billy?" she shrieks at me, her eyes bulging.

"Willam. I mean you and William! Sorry!"

I can hear my voice shaking. Is she really reacting to my calling him Billy? This is absurd! Totally crazy!

She's standing and leaning over the table with both hands flat on top of it scowling at me. I can feel my mouth hanging open as I stare at her.

"What the hell do you think you're saying? Don't try to psychoanalyze me Brooke. Save that shit for your bloody psychiatric patients! I'm not one of them! I'm not some paranoid, wacko nut! Some stupid, hopeless head case that you think you can shrink and make better," she snarls.

"Kylie. Please sit down. Please! I didn't mean to interfere between you and Bi...William. It's only a suggestion. I meant it to be helpful. Please. Sit down. And let's talk. We're friends, remember?"

She slowly sits down and takes a knife and starts to angrily cut the rest of her croissant into tiny pieces as I watch her. She's avoiding eye contact with me but she seems to be calming down. My mind is swirling. I've never seen Kylie react that way before. This is new behaviour. It's totally out of character for her. What's going on with her? Maybe Billy is right about all of this.

I clear my throat and force myself to smile slightly. I take a deep breath and sit back in my chair.

"Thanks for staying, Kylie. Look I'm really sorry. I didn't mean to offend you in any way. I'm only trying to be helpful. Really, I'm very sorry. I apologize," I say quietly.

"Just keep the therapy gobbledygook to yourself. OK? Not everybody is you, you know! As a matter of fact. Forget it Brooke! Let's just call it a day!" she snaps at me.

Kylie glares at me and throws down her knife. It clatters and bounces off of the side of her plate on to the edge of the table and then clanks on to the hard tile floor.

She jumps up and reaches down and pulls her purse on to her shoulder, turns her back on me and strides towards the entrance. Her purse is still wide open.

I stare at the knife and then back at her as she pulls open the door and walks out slamming the door with a bang. I watch her through the window as she half runs and half walks down the street. I can feel my heart hammering away in my chest.

CONSTANCE LECHMAN

Chapter Twenty-Three

"Hi Brooke. Look I'm sorry. I feel really terrible about the other day. I... I don't know what got into me. Hormones, I guess! I hope you're not too angry with me," Kylie says in a soft, hesitant voice.

"It's OK Kylie. We all get upset at times," I say. "I'm so glad that you called."

I'm in my office at the hospital in between patients and when I saw Kylie's name pop up on caller ID I picked up immediately. She sounds more like the Kylie I know, although a more tepid version. Not her previous strong, self assured self. But sane. At least she sounds sane today. Hormones? She's never talked about hormones bothering her before. In fact, she's always pooh poohed menopause, saying that she would never let it catch her. That was Kylie! This new version? A total stranger!

"It's not like me to lose it and certainly not with you Brooke. Not after all these years. Can I make it up to you by inviting you over to lunch on Sunday? We'll have a late lunch. I'll make a nice salad and some pasta. You always like my spaghetti primavera. What do you say? Is around 1:00 pm OK for you?"

"That sounds wonderful Kylie. I'll bring the wine! I've gotta go now. I have a patient who will be here any second," I say smiling and breathing a sigh of relief.

As I put my cell phone down on my desk I hear a knock at the door. I look at my watch. It must be Deborah Jones. It's exactly the time for her session. She's usually a couple of minutes late, but today she's right on time. I stand up and go to the door. I open it to a pacing, scowling Deborah who quickly brushes by me, taking her blazer off as she marches to the chair across from mine. I barely have time to sit down before Deborah starts talking and waving her hands around with every sentence.

"I can't believe it. He's trying to tell me that it meant nothing to him. It was just a mental lapse of some kind. To him maybe! And it was all her. Her fault! Really? Can you believe that? She seduced him. Yeah right! He says that he still loves me and he doesn't want to lose me. Well, it's a little late for that! What did he think? That he could have both of us? Her and me. That I'd be there to cook and take his clothes to the dry cleaner and maybe be good enough for an occasional roll in the hay when she was unavailable?" she says, finally pausing to take a breath.

"How are you feeling right now?" I ask an obviously enraged Deborah.

"Pissed off! Really pissed!" she hisses, clenching her fist in the air.

"Pissed off? Do you notice how you always have to qualify your feelings?" I comment.

"Oh shit! OK. I could kill the bastard! He's not getting away with this. If he thinks he can go scot free with an apology and some bloody flowers he can forget it!" she snaps.

"Do you see that you are using a bunch of words? How do you feel inside? Right now."

"Anger. I feel angry! I'm furious! Bloody furious!" she growls.

"Let's look at how you're experiencing that fury at your husband right now."

As Deborah relates her feelings and is obviously, finally, after three intensive therapy sessions, very in touch with them, I think about my anger towards Ryan for leaving me.

I'm helping Deborah to get in touch with her anger, when I was so unaware of my rage until getting into therapy with Lou Grimes. Chiron! My heart skips a beat as I picture the astrologer pushing her bright red glasses back up to the bridge of her nose.

And I really have to give Lou full credit. He was able to get through my buffer zone right into where my feelings are secreted away in hiding!

Because now I know that it's been like a burning volcano inside of me laying low, smoking, ready to erupt.

And what about Kylie? She's full of anger at Billy, but I don't even know if that anger is warranted. Billy isn't angry. And neither is Ryan!

Chapter Twenty-Four

"Damn it! What's going on?" I say to the closed door, looking at my watch again.

It's 1:20 pm and I've been ringing the doorbell and knocking on Kylie's front door, but with no response. I take a couple of steps back and look at the number. How stupid! I don't need to check the address! Of course I'm at the right door. I've been here a hundred times! But why isn't she answering it? I've tried her on my cell and her phone is turned off. Why would she turn her phone off if she's gone out? And why wouldn't she call me to tell me that she's going to be late? She's the one who suggested lunch at her place. Oh my God! Did I get it wrong? She did say her place didn't she? Yes! She said that she'd make pasta primavera! Didn't she?

Is she sitting in a restaurant somewhere waiting for me? No! That's impossible. She'd be texting or calling me to find out where I was. She must have forgotten! Why didn't I call earlier and confirm? I've never done that before. I've never had to confirm. But I guess I needed to this time because she's not here.

Maybe she forgot an ingredient or needed something and she's gone out for it and somehow got delayed. Or maybe she got into a car accident. Oh my God! Is that what happened? A car accident! I'll wait a few more minutes and then I'll start checking with friends to see if they've heard from her. She couldn't have just disappeared!

This wouldn't happen to the old Kylie. She was always on top of everything. A perfect hostess, a good doctor and now a best-selling writer, she doesn't just forget or ignore her commitments. I put the bag with the bottle of wine down on the front steps and take some tissues out of my purse and try to wipe the concrete step. The tissue shreds so I take out some more and pile them on top of each other on the step and I sit down on my makeshift covering to wait for her.

I see a familiar car pull up into the driveway. It's Billy's car? Why is Kylie driving his car? The driver's door opens and Billy gets out. I stand up and dust my pants off.

"Brooke! What are you doing sitting there like that?What's wrong?" Billy says with a surprised look.

"I'm waiting for Kylie. She invited me for lunch at 1:00 pm, but she's not here. And it's almost 1:30 pm now. Billy what's going on? Why are you here? She said that you'd left her for another woman!"

I think she told me that Billy had left. She was ranting so much that now I'm not sure exactly what she said. I guess I just assumed that he was gone. Because now that I think about it, she just said that he was having affairs.

He puts his hands in his pockets and looks down at the pavement and then back at me.

"She's probably home Brooke," he says, removing his sunglasses. "You'll see."

"Then why doesn't she answer the door? Besides, I called her on my cell and there's no answer. I'm worried. It's not like her. Something awful must have happened to her!"

"Yeah. Well. I'm pretty sure that she's here. It's just the same old shit. The usual. Nothing's changed," he mumbles looking down at the concrete driveway.

I stare at him as he pulls his keys out of his jacket pocket. He looks at me with a defeated air.

"Come on. I'm sure that I'm right. You'll see," he says walking towards the front door.

My stomach is tightening as I follow him into the house. The TV is blasting out a popular talk show somewhere in one of the rooms. No wonder she didn't hear the doorbell! As we enter the living room I see Kylie sprawled out on the sofa.

"Oh my God! Something's wrong," I say running over to her.

"No. She's asleep," Billy says standing in the doorway.

"Asleep?" I ask as I lean over her.

"She's out of it Brooke. Completely," he says shaking his head as he walks over to the TV and turns it off. "She's stoned all the time now. No matter what I say to her or how often she says that she's going to quit. I turn my back and she's doing it again. She's hooked. Sorry, I thought you knew that!"

Knew! That she's on drugs? My mind is blank. I feel paralyzed. Unable to move or think. Billy is standing next to me. I look up at him. He looks at me and raises his eyebrows and shrugs his shoulders. I see tears running down his face.

"I can't deal with it any more Brooke. I don't know what to do. When she's not stoned now, she's paranoid, saying that I'm cheating on her. That I hate her! And I'm lying to her. I'm not Brooke! Honest! I thought you knew. She said that she was going to tell you. She said that she was going to come clean with you and ask you to get her some help. She didn't? Right?"

"No. She didn't tell me. I had no idea. Oh Billy. When did this happen? When did all of this start?"

He motions to me to sit down in one of the wing chairs that face the coffee table and sofa. He sits in the other chair and turns to look at me shaking his head.

"Gradually. For a while now. You know Kylie liked her wine. And you remember when she fell and hurt her shoulder? And she was in so much pain? And then she had to have surgery to fix her rotator cuff?"

"Yes. Of course. But I thought that it got fixed. She had surgery for it," I say in a whisper,

"I don't know why or what happened. She went to physiotherapy for weeks before surgery and then when they decided to operate she went after that too for awhile. And I saw her doing some prescribed exercises at home. But she was always in pain. So she started with wine every night at dinner. But after a while one or two glasses weren't enough. And I was pretty sure that she was drinking during the day too."

"Oh my God Billy. I had no idea. I'm sorry, but somehow we just lost contact with each other for awhile and I just didn't know," I say. "I'm so sorry Billy."

He rubs his eyes and moans. For a few seconds he stares at Kylie and then turns back to look at me.

"Uh, well after that the doctor had given her a prescription for some pain killers and you know at first she was careful. But when the wine didn't seem to do it. I, uh. I noticed that she was still taking the pills. When I asked her about it. She got mad. Really angry. I thought the pills were only for a week or two weeks maybe. But she kept seeing that doctor and he kept renewing the prescription. And now she's hardly ever sober or clean or whatever the fucking word is. Sorry Brooke.

Whatever the word for it is."

He leans forward in the chair and puts his head in his hands and sobs. I stare at him and then at Kylie. She's snoring lightly. She's wearing a soiled, rumpled long sleeved T-shirt and wrinkled, baggy jeans. Her hair is greasy and stringy looking and she doesn't have on any makeup. This is not like the beautiful Kylie that I used to know who loved fashion and who was always so meticulous in her appearance.

My God how did this happen? Of course I know from my work at the clinic that it happens all the time. Pain killers! Over prescribing by doctors! It's an epidemic right now. And a very dangerous and silent killer!

But to Kylie? To my friend! Now I know why we lost contact for a while. I was so caught up in my problems with Ryan that I didn't know what she was going through. How awful! I've been a total failure to her! I feel tears start to trickle down my face.

Chapter Twenty-Five

"My mother always said to me, let's cuggle. That was her word for it. You know a big hug and a cuddle at the same time," he says with tears running down his face.

I'm with Mark and we're reviewing his early life with his mother memory by memory. At the start of the session he told me that he's eating normally, sleeping better and he's now able to concentrate on his studies. So I'm feeling very pleased with our progress.

Suddenly, Kylie's face slips into my mind and I get a huge knot in my stomach. Poor Kylie! And poor Billy! What a terrible mess they are in now. I know getting free of drugs, especially opiates, is incredibly difficult. Some people never do it. Instead, they end up dead in a deserted alley after a heroin or fentanyl overdose. I shudder at the picture of Kylie sprawled in a seedy, lonely laneway. She'll need a residential treatment centre if she's going to be able to overcome this addiction. Will she accept that? Right now, I don't think so. I don't think she's there yet. The knot in my stomach twists and tightens.

I need Ryan now more than ever. He was always my go to confidante. I loved him and trusted him. I told him everything. Especially something like this. He was never judgemental. He would understand my worries and be able to help me gain perspective and calm my anxiety with just a few words and a great big hug. A "cuggle!"

I never felt alone after Ryan came into my life. I picture him smiling in his beautiful long, black cashmere winter coat. In the summer he wears a wonderful Panama hat to protect him from the hot, overbearing sun. The brim really shows off his beautiful eyes. He always looks so handsome in everything he wears. I was always so proud to be seen with him. I sigh. At least he's still alive. Even if he'll never hug me or comfort me any more. Tears spring up in my eyes. I can't believe that I'll never see him smile at me again.

Our deal! We took that oath to never let the other one suffer. I feel a wave of grief well up. It's better to die instead! I need to kill myself! I can't go on like this without him.

Mark wipes his eyes with a wad of tissue. He grabs another handful and wipes the tears from his cheeks and chin.

"My mother had the best laugh. She really laughed. You know, she never held back," he says nodding and smiling at me.

I nod. I do know! Ryan was like that too! He could laugh. My throat constricts and I feel the tears threatening at the corners of my eyes.

"If I could just see her laugh just one more time! Just once more. That's what I wish for," he says reaching for a tissue to blow his nose and then shakes his head. "I'd give anything to see that!" He stares at me. "But it's good that I can still picture it. Right?"

I nod. I know exactly how it feels. My heart aches right now. But he's right it's good to have the memory. What does everyone say again? That it's better to have loved and lost than never loved at all? So stupid! Totally stupid! And so wrong.

"What will happen if I forget? If I forget what she looked like?" he says and starts to sob. "That can't happen. Ever!" he grits his teeth as he says it. "I won't let myself forget her face!" he announces, wiping his eyes with the back of his hand.

I won't either. I can't forget Ryan. Never! I'll never let myself forget him! I hold on to the arms of my chair tightly with both hands in order to push back the tears.

Chapter Twenty-Six

"So all in all, I'm feeling much, much better," I say shifting my body weight to get more comfortable in the chair across from Lou.

Chiron's wounds are healing. I won't tell Lou about Chiron because he'll think that I'm nuts. But, I will tell him that I want to take a break for awhile.

I can always come back if I feel the need to talk to him again.

"You start today's session by telling me that you're feeling better," he interjects. "And, you say that you're sleeping better and coping better at work, because you're less irritable and now you can concentrate. And you're getting good results with your patients. So they're doing well also. And you say that you have gained back the weight that you lost when you had no appetite. Yet," he pauses a moment, "you've never really told me why you became so depressed," he states and then pauses again. "More importantly, you have never specifically told me what you wanted help with when you came here," Lou says carefully enunciating his words.

His eyes are boring right into my face and into my brain. It's as if he is willing his eyes to actually drill deeply into the centre of my psyche, so he can see what I'm hiding from him. He's settled into his chair with his feet rooted firmly on the floor as usual.

Today, he's got on a pair of black New Balance sports shoes. They seem out of place with his black dress pants and the crisp white shirt and blue striped tie. Why running shoes when I'm the one on the run? Maybe he just doesn't look like a heavy duty private detective and he actually is one, and needs the shoes for chasing down the bad guys. Like me? Am I a bad guy?

Right now he looks completely immovable. Like a bulwark. I know that he won't budge until he gets what he's looking for from me.

"I. Well I, uh," my voice is shaking slightly and I have to clear my throat before I can speak. "You know. I told you about my husband, and uh, my best friend. I mean my husband is my best friend, and I still think that way about him. But I, I meant my best friend Kylie. You know I told you about her," my voice trails off as I end my sentence and I look down at the floor and back over to his shoes.

I'm babbling and I know that I'm not making any sense, even to me. What am I trying to say to him? I can feel a bomb forming inside of my core. What else can I say to get him to leave me alone? I have to stop him from probing and poking around inside of me. It's too horrible in there. No one can see it! Especially him!

"Well what am I supposed to say?" I snap at him.

My stomach is clenching and my heart is pounding so hard that I can actually hear it. What the hell does he expect from me? I've been exposing my guts to him. I've cried here more than I've thought that I could ever possibly cry in my life. Ever! Does he think that I've been faking it? Damn him! How dare he push me!

"Do you want blood from me!" I can feel my cheeks heating up as I spit the words out at him.

"Blood? You mention blood. Whose blood are you referring to?" he says calmly, emphasizing the word blood.

Shit! I raise my eyebrows and shake my head. I look away and out of the window at the tree outside. The sky is getting very cloudy. Big charcoal grey clouds. It looks like it will rain soon. My chest is starting to burn. Obviously it's anxiety. I know that much. I am a psychiatrist!

"I said it as a manner of speech. That's all. Not everything has a hidden meaning." I say sharply.

"Blood is simply a manner of speech? You know better than that Dr. Adams. You mentioned blood. And I asked you whose blood?"

He continues to stare at me. Impassive. Not moving. Patiently waiting. He has me trapped. I'm a rat in a cage. And I can't escape.

My body is charged with electricity. I want to jump up and run. What the hell is going on? Does he suspect something? How? How could he know? Ryan wouldn't have told him. He doesn't know Lou. And I certainly haven't told him. I've been very careful to say nothing about it. It's been difficult. But I haven't slipped. Not until now. Blood! Why did I say that? Damn it anyways! How did that leak out of me?

"I'm sorry I said it," I whisper looking at the clouds as they gather together and darken from charcoal to black.

It will rain soon. No it will pour! And I don't have an umbrella. I didn't bring a raincoat either. So I'll get drenched. Soaked.

"You're sorry? Why? Why are you sorry? And why do your eyes avoid me?" Lou drills.

He's watching and knows every move that I make. And he's relentless. He won't stop now. He smells blood. Like a lion! Why did I start this whole thing with him? What did I think that I was going to accomplish by going into therapy, while at the same time holding back on what is really killing me inside? Trying to hide the centre of my despair! The thing that I can't come to grips with now and maybe never!

I lean back and my head rests against the padded back of the chair. It feels like I'm not breathing, but I am, because my chest is moving. I close my eyes and feel the tears trickle down my cheeks. I take a deep breath and pull a wad of tissue out of the bottom of the sleeve of my cardigan and wipe the tears away.

"This blood that you identified is causing you a lot of pain. Isn't it?" he asks in a very gentle voice.

I start to nod and then stop. I blow my nose and take a big sigh.

"I don't know what you mean," I say quietly, staring him in the eyes.

Chapter Twenty-Seven

"No Ryan! No! No! Don't! Please stop! Stop!" I scream as I raise my hands over my head to try to grab his arms and stop him from slashing my face with what looks like some kind of a large butcher's knife.

As he plunges the steel blade into my mouth the blood squirts out and runs down my chin and neck soaking my chest!

I jerk awake! My face, hair, neck and breasts are drenched in perspiration. I wipe some of the dampness away with the palms of my hands and then dry them on the sheets.

Another nightmare! The same one! Again! I've had it every night since my last session with Lou Grimes. It's always the same basic nightmare except for one difference each time. The one constant is that Ryan is attacking me with a knife and there is always blood everywhere!

I'm panting so I take a deep breath and hold it in counting to ten. Then I release it and do it again. As

I start to relax my body, the panting subsides, I wriggle further down under the covers.

The first time I had the nightmare Ryan stabbed me in the middle of the forehead. The next night he stabbed me in the throat. This time it was the mouth! Three nights and three different targets. He's always standing over me and I'm completely helpless! Unable to fight him off.

What does it mean? And it's only after I mentioned the word blood to Lou Grimes in my session with him. Blood! I shiver as I say it. Why did I let that word escape out of my mouth? Damn it!

And why did Ryan stab me in my mouth last night? Because I said blood? And why stab me in my throat? Because I was telling Lou? And then in my forehead. Is it because of the idea, the very thought of blood! That has to be it! Thinking and talking about blood! But Ryan doesn't want to kill me. I feel dead because I've lost him. He is the one who has died in my life. Not me! I'm still alive. At least for now. I shiver and wriggle even deeper, pulling on the covers and wrapping them tighter around my torso.

I really don't want to have to share all of this garbage with Lou. Even though I know that I should. That's classic resistance on my part. All patients in therapy unknowingly resist exposing their worst unconscious conflicts. It's the therapist's work to get to them and expose them.

This is different. This would be more like active suppression on my part. Knowingly not telling him something that is significant and emotionally loaded is suppressing or holding back important information that could lead to a breakthrough in my therapy. So if I don't tell Lou about it, then I'm screwing up. I'm really defeating myself. Especially since it's a recurring nightmare. So of course I'm not helping myself by doing that. I can only benefit if I tell him. But then he'll delve head on into it and find out everything that I'm concealing from him. Unless. Unless I can tell him. Get his take on it. And only go so far. Except, he has a way of getting under and around my defences. So I should really stop seeing him.

I turn over and look at the clock. Oh no! It's 5:56 am! Damn it! The alarm is set for 6:00 am. I sigh. I need to get up and shower and get ready to go to work. I take a few more deep, slow breaths and close my eyes.

The image of Ryan holding the knife over my face flashes through my mind again. Oh my God! It's the chef's knife from our kitchen. I've had that knife for the entire time of our marriage. It was a wedding present from a friend of ours who was a young chef in training at the time. He proudly selected a high quality knife that would last us a lifetime. I've carefully looked after that knife, honing it with a sharpening steel after every use and I get it professionally sharpened once a year.

We've carefully moved it with us from place to place. We both love food and to cook and that knife has always been so precious to both of us. Talk about symbolic!

I shudder and throw off the top sheet and then the blanket and slowly swing my legs over the side of the bed onto the soft rug on the floor. I push the off button on the alarm and I take a deep breath, and then I stand up.

CONSTANCE LECHMAN

Chapter Twenty-Eight

"Thank you Dr. Adams. Thank you so much. I couldn't have done it without you. I was drowning before I came here," Mark says smiling at me. "I don't know what would have happened to me if I hadn't come here. So thank you for everything!"

He's a changed young man. Relaxed, energized and smiling. This was a classic case of crisis intervention therapy in a well functioning person with an acute grief reaction. Mark had good character strengths from having had a very positive significant relationship with his mother.

I'm smiling inside as I listen to him telling me about the changes in his mood and how he is now able to think about his mother without collapsing in grief. He's also doing well at university and in his relationship with his girlfriend.

"Let's look at what was helpful to you in our sessions and at what was not helpful," I say to him.

This is our last scheduled session and I always do a review to allow the patient to see the work that they've done, the progress they've made and how we've accomplished our goals. It gives them a strong, positive idea of how they can continue to do their own emotional and psychological work using the same tools that we used in our sessions. It gives them confidence as well as practical takeaways for their own use in the future.

After Mark's session I sit down at my desk and open my laptop to make the final notes on his case. We've agreed that he will call for a return appointment in three months to do a follow up review and I'm certain that he'll still be well. I enter the projected follow up date on his file and close the laptop.

I stand up and look out the window. I feel so lucky to have a window in my office even if it's not the greatest view. My heart stops! I see an elderly couple walking across the spacious parking lot holding hands. They're still in love! Watching them, I burst into tears. I collapse back down into my chair. Will this grief at losing Ryan ever stop?

It's been over an hour since I've checked for messages so I know that there will be several waiting. I take a deep breath before I pick up the office landline and tap in the code to access my voicemail. My pulse starts to race when I hear that Billy has called twice. That's unusual. I don't think he's ever called me on that phone line before. And it's especially odd, since there are no actual messages from him. That's weird! There must be a problem with Kylie. She texted me yesterday that she had been attending an outpatient group therapy drug treatment program. I was positive in my comments to her, but concerned because I really think that she needs an intensive residential program, where she can be closely supervised and monitored and where she is not able to get her hands on any drugs or alcohol.

I dial Billy's number and he answers on the first ring.

"Brooke! Thank you for calling me back," he says quickly.

"Hi Billy. I know that you've been trying to reach me. And I'm sorry it took me awhile to call you back, but I was in a session with a patient. Is everything OK? Is there a problem with Kylie?"

"No. She's doing better. She started the group stuff. She went yesterday again and she's going to go this evening. I called because, well I uh, I went to see Ryan. And well, I hadn't seen him in awhile. I was surprised, Brooke. Shocked. Sorry to say it, but he's not doing well. Sorry, but I guess you must know that. I. I, uh needed to touch base with you. I hope you don't mind my saying this," he says.

A sharp stabbing sensation slices through my chest, right where my heart is. My Ryan! What should I do? What can I do? How can I help him?

"Thanks Billy. Thanks for telling me. And thanks for reaching out to him," I say quietly. "I appreciate your concern and it's good to hear that Kylie is taking the group program seriously. I really hope that it helps her. I'll give her a call tomorrow to see how she's doing."

"Uh. That's not all. Uh. I uh don't think so Brooke. I mean that's really also why I wanted to talk to you. To kind of, you know, to give you a head's up. I didn't know if I should or not but," he pauses. "Well, she's really angry at you."

"At me? Why? What did I do?" I mutter.

Just what I need. What the hell is he saying? When it rains it always pours. It's just one damn problem on top of another in my personal life,

"Yeah, well. She blames you Brooke. She says that it's your fault that she got this bad into the drugs. You're a doctor and a psychiatrist and she says that you should have known that she was in trouble and you should have helped her. She thinks that you should have seen the signs and intervened somehow to stop her from getting addicted."

"But I didn't know!" I sputter as I pull the receiver away and look at it.

Am I really crazy? What is Billy saying? I'm not a mind reader. Yes. I've been preoccupied, but I can't know everything about everybody! And I'm not everyone's therapist! Therapist to the world? Hell, I'm having a hard time holding it together for myself!

"Do you agree with her? Do you think so too Billy? Please be honest with me. I need to know," I say gritting my teeth.

Hell. She's a doctor too. She knows about this shit. She knows how bloody easy it is to get addicted to painkillers. It's a bloody epidemic now. She's not some innocent in all of this. What the hell was she doing letting this get so out of control?

"No of course not. I mean, she's the one who got addicted. I wanted her to tell you about it a long time ago. But she wouldn't and she wouldn't let me say anything to you. She said that she'd conquer the problem and then everything just went off the rails and it was too late. I think working at home alone, you know, writing, wasn't the best thing in this situation. Anyways I wanted you to know. I thought that I should warn you. I'm sorry," he says as his voice trails off.

"OK. Yeah. Thanks Billy, I appreciate your call. I'll, I'll talk to you soon. Bye for now," I say and I slam the receiver down to end the call. I slowly put my head down on my desk and start to sob.

Chapter Twenty-Nine

"My husband is acting in a completely different way towards me these days. I barely recognize his new attitude. And he seems genuinely happy! And I realize that it's because of me. It's because I've changed! So he has had no choice! He had to change too!" Deborah Jones says with a smile.

"I feel like I'm a different person now. I know my feelings and I'm not afraid to say what I feel and he is listening to me. Before coming here to see you Dr. Adams, I realized that I used to be angry, but I held it in and I didn't say anything about how I felt and then I ended up resenting him. And he knew it. He could feel it. And he resented me back. It was like a Mexican standoff!"

"So you say that now you are in touch with your anger and you are able to speak to him about it and he is able to respond differently to you?" I repeat back to her.

"Yes! I was always afraid to say what I felt before. Especially anger. But not only anger. Even my love for him. Now I can tell him that I love him and he responds to that too! I know that we, I, have a long way to go, but I'm different now and that means that we're different as a couple! It's amazing! Really amazing!!" she says nodding excitedly at me as she talks.

I feel my cell phone vibrate in my blazer pocket partway through our session. I can feel an unease start inside of me. It's obviously not related to my work with Deborah, which is going better than I could have ever thought possible. She's turned out to be a dream patient making big strides very quickly.

So I must be feeling something ominous related to the phone call. Because most of the people that I know don't call me during the day. They know that I'm working. Patients call me on the land line in my office. So whoever it is really wants to get in touch with me urgently. I wonder who it is? I'm feeling antsy, so as soon as Deborah leaves I'll look at who was calling me.

As I close the door on Deborah I pull my cell phone out of my pocket and look at the missed call. Billy! What the hell? It's been over a week since we spoke. Why would he be calling me today? I tap on the screen and hear the ring on his end. He picks up immediately.

"Brooke! Is she with you?"

"She? You mean Kylie?" Why would Kylie be with me? She's angry at me and has been ignoring my calls and messages for several days.

"Yes of course I meant Kylie. Is she with you?" he says irritably.

"No. She isn't answering my calls. So no. I haven't spoken to her since you and I talked. Why? What's happened?"

"She didn't come home last night. I have no idea of where she is. I called the rehab centre and they haven't seen her in three days. She hasn't been going there any more. Where has she been going when she leaves the house? Where is she Brooke?" Billy's voice cracks.

"Oh my God Billy. I don't know. Have you tried some of her other friends?"

"What other friends? You're the only one who has stuck by her. She pissed everyone else off because she never kept up with them and she was hiding at home drinking and well you know," he says and groans as he talks. "You were the only one that she kept in contact with Brooke."

I hear his voice catch and it sounds almost like he's panting.

"Billy are you OK?"

"No Brooke. No I'm not OK. This is hopeless!" he says, starting to sob. "What should I do? How can I find her?"

"When you spoke to the rehab centre did you ask them who she was friendly with in the group? Is there someone, maybe another client in the group, who might know where she is? Maybe she said something about her plans there in one of the sessions?"

"I asked and they checked with the group therapist and apparently there's someone else who didn't return. Someone she was seen having coffee with after the group meeting," he says sobbing again. "Oh Brooke!"

"Who? Maybe you can get her phone number and she'll know where Kylie is. Maybe Kylie's with her."

"No Brooke. No. It's not like that."

"No she's not with her?"

"No!" he says in a whine and then sighs deeply. "It's a man. A man! Not a her. She must be with him!" he barely gets the words out. He's crying so hard.

"Oh shit!" I sputter and then put my hand over my mouth.

"Yeah. Shit!" he moans. "Oh Brooke. I was worried that I'd find her laying in a back alley somewhere, but I didn't think that she'd just leave me for someone else. Some other guy!"

I nod my head, and clear my throat. I know this happens all the time. Two people who are struggling emotionally, cling to each other as the solution to their problems and as a way to avoid dealing with their real issues. And it's especially true of addicts. But, in the end all they're doing is making everything worse. They think they've found true understanding, their soulmate and true love, but it's just another escape hatch, another crutch instead of finally dealing with their problems. But Kylie? This can't be real!

"Yeah! I'm, I'm stunned Billy," I manage to say. "I'm completely shocked. Of course we don't know if that's what has actually happened. We really don't know that she's run off with some man. And you know Billy if she has, then it's better than finding her in a back alley, even if it doesn't feel that way. It is better. This way the two of you can still work things out. It's never too late."

"Yeah right!" he snaps. "What am I going to do? Just wait? Sit and wait and hope that she comes back home, to me?"

"Look, I'll call our emergency room and check to make sure that she's not been brought in there.

Why don't you call the police and let them know. I don't know what they can do at this point. But if there's been an accident. I assume that she has her car. Right? So maybe there's been an accident? And, and this other rehab group patient? This guy. Did they tell you his identity?"

"No. I was so upset. So shocked that when they told me about him, well I was yelling Brooke. And I lost it and they just said that they couldn't tell me anything. They said it was confidential information. Shit!" I can hear him blow air out and moan slightly.

"Yeah, I'm not surprised Billy. About the confidentiality part I mean. Damn! If we only knew who he was it might help us to find her," I mumble.

"She does have her car though. So it's a good idea to call the police. I'll call them right away. And then I'll go there to the rehab place and talk to them in person and see if I can get a name and a phone number for this guy," he rattles out. "Oh Brooke!" he says with another moan.

"I know Billy. I'm so sorry. I feel terrible about all of this. And I know that you do too," I say almost whispering.

"Yeah. Thanks Brooke," his voice trails off in an utterly defeated sounding way.

"Billy please let me know if you hear anything at all and I'll do the same. I have to go because I have another appointment scheduled. But I'll check with the staff in the ER first. If I have any news I'll call you back right away."

My mind is whirling with thoughts about Kylie and the image of her crumpled up, helpless, and alone in some skid row drug house sets my pulse racing. I can't believe what's happening to my friend! What is happening? Where is she? Is she really with another man? He's an addict too! Is he dangerous? Has something terrible happened to her? Has he hurt her? How can this be happening to Kylie and Billy?

I've already lost Ryan and now maybe Kylie! My two best friends!

Chapter Thirty

"Our friend Billy. Uh. Umm. Billy, he's a mutual friend of both my husband, of, of both of us. He's known Ryan for years. Actually, Billy and Kylie and Ryan and I, we all go back together to university days. He. Uh, well he saw Ryan recently and he told me that he was shocked by the change he saw in him," I say to Lou Grimes and then take a deep breath.

I can hear my heart pounding. My throat starts to tighten and I have trouble breathing. It feels like someone has put their hand over my mouth and nose and I can't get enough air in or out. I uncross my legs and push my feet into the rug on the floor. I stare at Lou. How much can I say? How far can I go without slipping and telling him everything? I feel like a huge wave is washing over my head and I'm drowning. To save myself all I need to do is reach out and grab hold of the lifeline that Lou is throwing to me, but my arms won't move. My legs are like concrete blocks. And my mouth is so dry that I can't open it. It's stuck shut. I look out of the window that's spotted with rain and watch the tree branch sway in the wind.

I know that I should reach out, but I can't lift my arm because it's too hopeless. There is no real lifeline here for me. One way or another there is no hope. No solution to this overwhelming problem. Not if I still love Ryan. I picture what he looked like when I visited him in the hospital a few months ago. He was amazingly lucid that day. So much so, that I was stunned.

He'd talked coherently. He'd said, if you love me, you'll do it. For me. For us! For what we've always been together, the two of us. And he'd reminded me that we had a deal. A real contract! He kept saying that we'd always been a team! He was begging me, saying please, and that as a doctor I could start now and slowly prescribe the right combo for him. I could make a pill cocktail for him. He said that he couldn't go on like this. That it was inhuman! He asked me to promise him that I'd do it, if I loved him because I was his only hope. His eyes were pleading with me and his hand was clinging tightly to my arm.

He's right we did make a deal. At first I thought that it was funny because we were so young and healthy. We'd talk about it like it was something so far away that it was just harmless, aimless chatter between us. Yet, we both swore that we'd do it for the other if we ever got to the point that we couldn't recover from an illness. We didn't want medical heroics only to lay in a hospital bed until we shrivelled up and died. We wanted it to be our decision. Our way. And now he's so much worse. He's a shell now. And Billy confirmed it when he visited him. So it's not my imagination.

Lou shifts in his chair and I stare at him. What does he think?

"I'll never forget the first time that Ryan didn't recognize me," I say in a raspy voice that doesn't sound like it's coming from inside of me.

I didn't intend to speak. But it has to be my voice. There's only the two of us here in this room. I slowly look around at the books in the bookcase, at his desk, at the window, and then at the rug on the floor.

Lou is silent, staring at me. He's wearing the same tie that he had on the last time that I was here. It's a burgundy and fuchsia striped silk. I shift in the chair and sit up straighter and square my shoulders and look him in the eyes.

"He'd been increasingly forgetful since the accident. Little things. You know. Always misplacing his keys. Forgetting to do an errand that he'd promised me that he would do. And before the accident he never forgot anything. That's why he was so good in court. Then it, it got worse. Forgetting names of people and of things. I'd find him staring at a simple object like his wallet, as if he was trying to figure out what it was," I say taking a deep breath.

I hesitate. Maybe I should stop. But the pain in my chest is suffocating me. I need to get some of this out.

"He'd been working part time only. Then one day I got a call from his senior partner Glen, who said that they didn't mind him coming into the office for a coffee or for a visit with his colleagues. He could do that, they were sympathetic, being nice, but they couldn't give him any new cases. They had already transferred his caseload to another lawyer. Glen asked me what the neurologist was saying about his prognosis. I knew then that things were unravelling. We were on the proverbial slippery slope. And going downhill very fast!

I sigh and look at Lou who is watching me. His forehead is furrowed. He remains quiet.

"I remember that I was paralyzed with fear and after the call from his law partner was over, minutes later I was still holding the phone, totally unable to move. I didn't know what to do!" I say breaking into tears.

"You said that you remember the first time that he didn't recognize you?" Lou says quietly.

"One day," I say and pause. "When I went to visit him and, and I uh walked into his room and he was sitting up in a chair. And they had him strapped in so he wouldn't fall out and he just looked right through me. I spoke to him, but he didn't speak. He didn't acknowledge me. He didn't even look to see who I was," my voice cracks. "He just sat there as if I wasn't even in the room. It was a shock, because I knew then that he didn't know me. It broke my heart," I say as tears roll down my face. "I mean I knew he had brain damage," I say banging my fist on my knee. "But I thought over time that he would grow out of it," I say wiping my eyes with the back of my hand.

"Grow out of it?" Lou asks.

It sounds ridiculous when I hear Lou echo my words. Absolutely ridiculous. I've been in denial. Full out denial. Of course, it was only going to get worse. Lesions! He had big brain lesions! Glen and the people in his office saw that. Billy saw the changes. And I was hiding my head in the sand. I look at Lou through the tears streaming down my face.

"I guess my philosophy for life must be that it's better not to know something when it's going to be bad news. It's better to live in the moment and not be miserable for too long. To live as long as possible in a protective bubble until someone or something bursts it," I say shaking my head. "Stupid!" I mumble as my father's face pops into my mind.

"Stupid?" Lou repeats. "You're not a stupid woman Dr. Adams!" he says softly.

I look at him. I slowly nod my head.

"Soon all I will have is a photograph of Ryan. That's all I have left of my father. Just a picture in a silver frame," I say quietly wringing my hands. "That's all I have left of anyone, my mother, my brother. All of them are gone!"

"So not only your mother and father. Now it's Ryan too. You've lost everyone that you have been attached to and loved dearly in your life. That's a lot of blood," he says.

I nod and blow my nose and wipe my face. He's right! I'm the only one alive! They're all dead. I'm a killer! I look out of the window. I need to escape. Get out of here.

"You're very quiet," he says.

The weight in my chest is becoming unbearable. I take a deep breath and shift in the chair to ease the painful pressure.

"I didn't want to ever think about it! For a long time the way that I coped was to try to just flow with it. Not think about them to avoid the pain. Not to experience my feelings, to keep afloat above them. Float over them," I say shaking my head and pointing my finger at the side of my head. "It was a hell of a way to live, because I was numb! But it helped me for a while. Crazy! Crazy me! What was I thinking?"

"Crazy?" Lou says quietly, staring at me and frowning.

I nod and sigh.

"He's gone so far down, completely deteriorated so fast. And now, in the last couple of weeks he's an empty shell. He doesn't recognize anyone now. Not Billy. Billy's been good about visiting pretty regularly," I say and nod my head. "And he doesn't know me. He doesn't even know the staff who are caring for him on a daily basis," I say and then wipe my eyes and cheeks. "I sit on his knee and hug him and kiss him and he doesn't move," I whisper, wiping my eyes again with my fingers. "He needs total care and full supervision. When I had to place him in a long term care hospital it broke my heart. But it was too much. I couldn't leave him alone, while I went out to work. And now I worry constantly, all the time, even though he's in a good place with excellent credentials. Still I worry that he will be neglected. And I can't bear thinking about that," I say with a sob that I try to hold back, but it's much stronger than me and it escapes from my throat.

"So you've been having thoughts that he will suffer there where you placed him?" Lou asks me.

"Yes. I think that no one will care for him the way I can or should. Worse than that," I sigh and shift in the chair. "I feel that I've abandoned him. And, sometimes I think that he knows me, you know, recognizes me still, because he'll close his eyes when I hug him. Maybe it's wishful thinking, but it breaks my heart," I say wiping my eyes again with my fingertips. "Because if he does know me somewhere deep inside of him then he knows that I've just dumped him. It's making me go crazy!" I say with another sob that forces its way out of me.

Lou stares at me and is silent for a few moments.

"Wishful thinking?" He finally says very slowly and in a voice so low that I strain to hear him.

I take a deep sigh and a squeaky sound comes out of my throat.

"Yes! I don't want him to be gone inside. And, most of all. Most of all I don't want him to suffer or to think that I've abandoned him when he needs me the most," I say while I reach over and grab a handful of tissues from the box on the table in front of me.

I wad them up into a ball and press it against my mouth. Tears are pouring out of my eyes and running down my face on to my neck and on to the collar of my white silk shirt as I stare at Lou.

"So is this what is causing you so much pain now? The thought that he might still be alive in some way?" Lou asks quietly. "That he's not dead inside?"

I nod at him before wiping the tears from my cheeks and under my chin. Is Lou a father? Does he have a daughter that loves him?

"Yesterday morning, they called me from the long term care hospital," I shudder as I speak. "I hate that term!" I whisper, sighing. "And, well this is crazy! They said he was having a good day and he was recognizing some of the staff. They asked if I wanted to come and take him out for a few hours. I was working. I had patients all day, and I can't just cancel them like that. So I said no," I shake my head as I speak. "No! How could I?" I say with tears in my eyes.

Lou is quiet, waiting for me. I take a deep breath. The back of my neck is aching. I run my hand over it to ease the tension.

"I felt terrible saying no. And, and I hate to say it, but it makes it worse. Is he alive inside or is he gone?" I say shaking my head again. "I don't know what to think or do any more!"

"So are you saying that you are helping everyone else, but not Ryan?" Lou asks me.

"Yes," I say nodding my head. "It's horrible! So, so terrible!" I whimper and my voice cracks as I say the word terrible.

"So you are in a terrible conflict over what to do. Is this the blood that you were referring to? You are afraid that you are killing Ryan? That he will die because you have completely abandoned him and he will be neglected and abused without you?"

I stare at him. My eyes, glassy from tears, feel like they are going to pop out of my face. I feel like I've stopped breathing. I look down at my chest to see if it is still moving. Am I alive?

"Yes!" I would prefer to be dead and let him be alive and OK again," I whisper.

"Yes?" Lou says, raising his eyebrows.

"It's better if he is dead," I say nodding my head. "Completely dead, not half dead! Especially the inside of him! The part of him that might know what's happening to him," I gasp out and covering my face with my hands I start to sob.

Chapter Thirty-One

"Hi Billy. Have you heard anything from Kylie? Is she OK?" I ask as I juggle my cell phone and the keys to my office door.

Of course she's OK. I'm stupid to be asking. But I haven't heard any news from either Billy or Kylie. And I didn't sleep well last night not hearing from them and wondering what's happened to her. I'm pretty sure that by now she's found her way back home and they've probably had it out and made up and forgotten to tell anyone.

I've just arrived at my office and I called him knowing that I have about ten minutes before I see the first scheduled patient, Mrs McCormick, a seventy year old woman who is scheduled for follow up after an evaluation session last week. I prescribed some anti-depressants and I want to monitor how she's doing with the medication.

I ease into my desk chair being careful not to spill the latté that I picked up at the Starbucks kiosk by the hospital entrance.

"No. Nothing Brooke. I haven't heard a thing from her," he says in a defeated tone.

"Nothing? But," I say as I feel myself freeze inside at the thought that she's still missing.

Nothing! This can't be happening! She can't have just disappeared!

"I'm going crazy worrying about her. I can't believe what's happened! That she's not here. I never slept all night. How could I? Where is she?" he asks and takes a deep sigh.

"Oh Billy. I, I can't believe it either. To think that she got herself in trouble with those damn opioids and now she's disappeared! And maybe with another, uh, patient. I see this at the hospital all the time, but not with my best friend! Not Kylie!"

"I called all her old friends. And I texted everyone in that friend circle group that you have and no one has heard from her! The police haven't found the car abandoned anywhere and I tried calling all of the hospitals around here, but nothing! There's not a sign of her anywhere!"

"What about the rehab group that she was attending? Were you able to ask any more about, about this, this other group member? Were they able to tell you anything about him at all?"

I can't bear to even repeat that it's a man! The thought of her running away with another man is still shocking to me. I hear a choking sound. Then Billy takes a deep breath.

"She. Apparently she started a friendship with this guy in the group. He's also a new member!" he says and chokes again as if he's stifling a sob. "So they don't know much about him. He. Oh! He's a heroin addict Brooke! Can you believe it? And he's also stopped attending. They both left at the same time. So it, it looks like they might have taken off somewhere together. And they won't tell me any more than that. Except they said that they asked and no one else in the group has seen either of them. Oh God Brooke! Why another man? What did I do wrong?"

"Nothing! You're not to blame. Nothing warrants this Billy. I really don't know. But obviously she's not thinking straight. It sounds like she was still taking drugs and denying it when she was going to the group. And, I'm sorry, but unless someone is strictly monitored they keep slipping back to the drugs. They're highly addictive. Doctors aren't supposed to keep on prescribing them. It's supposed to be a very short term treatment. That was very wrong of that damn doctor! It's no wonder that she got hooked! Her brain is now addicted and it craves the drugs."

"I should have stayed home with her. I should have stopped work and watched her. Not left her alone," he says.

"It's not your fault Billy. She needs locked treatment. That's hard to accept when you're an addict. But you couldn't stay home and guard her!

You can't watch someone 24/7. She would have found a way to sneak out and get the drugs that she was craving."

I hear a soft knock at my door. I look at my watch. It must be Mrs McCormick. She's five minutes early.

"I'm sorry. My first patient is here. So I need to start work. Please promise to call or text me if you hear anything. Anything at all. I'll keep my phone on vibrate and check for my messages."

"OK. I promise. Thanks Brooke. Uh, look there's just one thing before you go. It's been bothering me. I hope you don't mind that I keep visiting Ryan. I'm sorry if you aren't happy about it. But I was hoping that he would still know me and well at least I could say goodbye to him. I mean. Sorry. I wanted to try to talk to him while he still knew me."

"I know, And it's fine Billy. He's still your friend. And apparently he's been having some good days this past week," I say with a deep sigh.

"I miss him a lot. We used to do those power walks sometimes. And talk. He was, he is a great guy Brooke."

"Yeah! It's funny that you mention that. I. I was also thinking earlier when I was walking to work about all the walks that he and I used to take. Every weekend. Sunday mornings. We'd walk and talk nonstop. And we'd pick up fresh croissants and coffee from that little French bakery on our way home."

"I know I used to laugh when he'd tell me that, because every time you two would walk longer and farther and then he'd say that I would have to get in shape to keep up," he says chuckling.

"I loved it. We'd hold hands or I would hold his arm," I say catching my breath.

"I guess those were the good old days. In every way for all of us! This is such a strange conversation. I never thought that we'd be having it Brooke."

I nod and wipe away the tears that are slowly trickling down my face. Another knock! I forgot for a moment that there was someone waiting. I'm losing it! I stand up and take a couple of deep breaths.

"Who knew that this would happen? The last time we walked together he was holding on to my arm and taking baby steps. As if he didn't even know how to walk any more," I say quickly and sigh. "Now he's in a wheelchair and he doesn't speak. He hasn't said a word to me in weeks! He doesn't know how to speak any more! And now Kylie is missing!" I rattle off blotting the dampness on my face. "Sorry Billy, I really gotta go. Keep me posted. Please!"

I put my phone on vibrate and slip it into my jacket pocket and reach for a tissue to dab at the wet streaks under my eyes. I take a deep breath and push my shoulders back and walk to the door to open it. Chiron! The wounded healer. Maria was right all those years ago! This is who I am!

CONSTANCE LECHMAN

Chapter Thirty-Two

"Would you meet me later today for a drink Brooke, say around 5:30 pm or 6:00 pm?" Ryan asked me the day after I'd first met him. "Please say yes! I won't take a no from you!"

I pause and swallow hard as his words suddenly run through my mind. My heart starts to race. That beautiful voice of his!

"It was the first time that Ryan had called me for a date. And I'll never forget those exact words and the sound of his voice. My heart soared when I picked up the phone message that he had left me. It was actually the morning after the first time that we'd met. My hand was shaking when I tapped in his phone number. I was dying to see him again and the sooner the better! I couldn't wait. And a drink! A drink with a handsome man. Somehow it sounded so glamorous and it definitely felt exciting!"

I look at Lou to see his reaction to what I've just told him. He is looking at me so intently that I can't look away, and even though I want to avoid his eyes I can't. I shift in the chair and cross my legs. I'm aware that my arms are crossed around my chest. Defensive posture! I slowly release them and arrange them loosely on the arms of my chair. Lou is silent.

"These days he's all I think about. The only time I stop is when I'm working. Otherwise Ryan occupies every inch of my mind. All of my thoughts. I can't stop my mind from thinking about him," I say, fidgeting and doing my best to avoid looking directly at Lou.

"Would you like to tell me about that meeting for the drink? What did you like about him when you first dated him? What attracted you to him?" Lou asks quietly.

"Well, I met him at the Vogue Hotel bar and he was even more handsome than I remembered. I was in awe of his elegance and sophistication. He was wearing a dark charcoal grey suit with a white shirt and a fuchsia coloured silk tie. We ended up having two glasses of very expensive chablis. And we never stopped talking. It was amazing! We talked and talked! He graciously suggested dinner in the adjacent dining room and of course I agreed. I didn't want to stop talking to him. We had so much in common. We both loved the same music, the same movies and books. I still remember what we ate. Fresh oysters and smoked salmon to start and then a delicious hangar steak with the best french fries that I'd ever tasted. They were made with duck fat," I say smiling and feeling myself relax.

"You're talking about the wine and food that you liked so much. What did you like about him? What was so special about him? Why are you avoiding telling me?" he says, frowning.

"I think it was his energy. He was electric. And it was also as if there was an energy that flowed easily between us."

"What incident comes to your mind about this energy between you," he says.

"Well, I can picture him. I can see him now. It was after our third dinner date and Ryan came back to my condo for an after dinner espresso. I remember standing in my kitchen and flicking the on switch of the coffee machine. I turned to look at him and he was standing there smiling at me. I can still picture the scene perfectly," I say as my heart starts to speed up.

"What did you say to him?"

"I love this machine," I say laughing. "It was a silly thing to say. I remember telling him that and telling him that it was so much easier and cleaner to use the espresso pods than the way I used to do it. You know, before I would grind the beans, measure it out, and then finally after all that work you end up with a cup of coffee! That's exactly what I said," I say and swallow.

"And what did Ryan say?"

"Nothing. He stepped towards me and reached out and I clung to him. We stood hugging each other for several minutes. I moved my hands over his back. It was muscular, no fat! He smelled faintly of citrus. Like a perfect fresh combination of lemon, lime and orange. When we released each other, I can remember it as if it was yesterday. I remember I said to him that I knew that I had been talking to him, but at that moment I had no idea of what I had just said to him," I say with my heart hammering away as I look at Lou's eyes.

I can feel the love for Ryan swell up in me with a force so strong that I almost choke. I'm right there in the kitchen with Ryan. The real Ryan not the shell that he is now. I put my hand over my mouth.

Tears start to trickle out of the corners of my eyes.

"You're there now, with him in the kitchen. Aren't you?" Lou says quietly.

I press my fingers against my eyes and nod. I have to take several deep breaths to get some air inside of my lungs.

"Yes! We both laughed and hugged again," I say nodding. "As he released me, my left shoulder, the area that I had overstretched in yoga class a few days before, gave me a twinge and I jerked slightly. He was so concerned and so protective, insisting on giving my shoulder a gentle massage. Of course it felt like I was in heaven. A massage from an incredibly handsome and sophisticated man, who was both strong and amazingly sweet and gentle at the same time. That incident totally describes Ryan in a nutshell," I say tears streaming down my face.

"So he is very passionate and compassionate," Lou says.

I nod using a wad of tissue to dab at my eyes and cheeks.

"After that we were inseparable, dating whenever we could. We both had busy professional careers, but we always found time to talk every day and to see each other every weekend. We were married a year after we met. It was the happiest day of my life. And I've never regretted that decision for even one second. Ever!"

"And now?" he asks me.

"And now I have to learn to live without him. This is the hardest thing that I've ever had to do. I sigh and wad the tissue into a tighter ball in my fist. How? How can I live without my husband?" I say as my mind is whirring with the pictures of him pleading with me, begging me to help him stop all of his suffering.

A pain so strong that it takes my breath away slams into me and stabs me right in the middle of my chest. And suddenly as if a lightning bolt has struck me, my mind is clear!

Chapter Thirty-Three

"Hello Brooke. It's Melinda. Listen, I'm on duty in the ER and there's a patient that was brought in by ambulance about an hour ago. The social worker found your name and number in her address book in her purse. Her name is Kylie Alexander. The paramedics administered Naloxone on the scene, she revived and they got her here asap. She's resting comfortably right now. But, she's in bad shape Brooke. She was really out of it when she got here. Is she a patient of yours? Do you know anything about her drug taking history that could help us?"

"Oh my God Melinda! She's a long time friend. I know that she recently got hooked on opioids. What happened exactly? Is her husband Billy there with her?"

"No. We've called him and he's on his way. She's been using for a while Brooke. Looks like a probable heroin overdose. When the husband gets here the social worker Emily from our team is going to see him so we can get a decent psychosocial history and find out exactly what drugs she's been using. She was found unconscious in a hotel room and brought here. All we know is that whoever was with her panicked and called the hotel reception when she wouldn't wake up and they called 911. Apparently, the other person who was with her then took off so the hotel security was left holding the bag! The paramedics said that there was evidence of heroin use in the room."

"Thank goodness whoever it was at least called for help and didn't just abandon her. What a mess! Look I'm in the clinic seeing new out patients. But, it's almost noon and we're just about finished. I only need to look at the notes the team did on the charts and sign off on them. So I can come down to see her in about half an hour. Maybe less. Is that OK?"

"Sure Brooke. She's not going anywhere for a while. And like I said she's comfortable and sleeping right now anyway. We may have to admit her for a couple of days if there's a bed and if she's open to getting treatment. I've asked for a consult from the Addictions Unit Resident. I won't know any more until we get all of the blood test results and the urine toxicology screen back. I'll tell Emily that I've talked to you so she knows also because the husband might mention you since you're a friend."

"OK good. Thanks for calling and alerting me Melinda," I say.

"But, Brooke, we had a case like this last week, the patient left after we got him stabilized. And he was picked up and brought back 24 hours later by ambulance. I pronounced him dead on arrival!" she says.

"Yeah!" I say with a deep sigh. "I know. I'll talk to both her and her husband. They need to get her into treatment right away. Look. Thanks for calling me," I say and I end the call and put my cell into my lab coat pocket.

Melinda's right. The statistics aren't on Kylie's side. Most patients brought in to ER for opioid overdoses die within a year because of a relapse. My mind is swirling with images of Kylie as I start to look at the write ups on the patients our multidisciplinary team assessed this morning. How did this get so out of control and in what seems like such a short time? I know that Billy said that she'd been abusing the opioids for a while. Oh my God! How terrible! I can't believe that this is happening to her!

The team had lots of questions about one of the patients who presented with multiple social problems as well as schizophrenia so it takes us a little over an hour before we finish. I pick up my keys from the conference room table where I'd placed them and I put them into my lab coat pocket and start for the bank of elevators that will take me down to the emergency department. I can feel my stomach starting to flutter as I get closer.

When I arrive at the emergency waiting room I see Billy pacing and talking on his cell phone. I start to walk towards him. He looks up and sees me and waves. He taps his phone and pops it into his jacket pocket.

"Brooke! Thank God you're here. I need to see her. They told me that I have to wait to talk to the social worker first," he says with tears slipping down his cheeks.

I put my hand on his arm. He grabs me and hugs me.

"Let me go in and see if I can find either the psychiatrist or the social worker on duty. Give me a few minutes OK?"

"Yeah Brooke. Do you know anything? Is she OK?"

"She's in good hands Billy. And very safe right now. But she needs to get treatment. This is terribly serious."

He nods his head and sits down putting his head in his hands. I push open the door and enter the corridor and walk to the nursing station to try to locate Melinda or the social worker and to see exactly where Kylie is situated.

All of the patient's names are marked on a whiteboard by the nursing station and their location in the Emergency Room area is indicated. I see her name and bed location along with Melinda's name as the doctor responsible.

I walk over to where Kylie is lying. She's in the bed closest to the nursing station and the curtain encircling the bed is pulled back so she can be clearly observed by the staff as they work in the area around her attending to the other patients. A nurse that I've seen many times in the corridors, but don't know by name, and a psychiatry resident are with the patient in the next bed who appears to be psychotic. He's moaning and screeching that someone is boring holes into his head. The resident is administering an injection and the nurse is talking to the patient trying to soothe him. I wave at them and nod towards Kylie and the nurse nods back.

I pull the curtain closed around her bed and look at Kylie. Her eyes are closed and her mouth is open slightly. She looks so different. Wasted is the word that comes to my mind. She's skinnier and looks about ten years older. Her roots are showing. So unlike her. I reach over the side of her bed and touch her arm. Her eyes shoot wide open

"Brooke!" she sputters and starts to cry. "Oh Brooke! I'm sorry. So sorry! Oh my God! I've lost everything. Even Billy! What am I going to do now? He hates me!"

"He doesn't hate you Kylie. In fact, he's been frantic worrying about you. Actually, he's outside in the waiting room. He loves you and he wants to see you," I say as I put my hands on the bedside rail and look down at my friend.

Kylie's hair is unwashed and stringy and what little of her eye makeup that is left is streaky and smeared underneath, making her dark circles look even worse. She reaches for my hand and clings on to it.

"I need help Brooke. I need lots of it," she says in a hoarse voice staring at me.

Her eyes look huge and full of fear. I squeeze her hand and brush a strand of hair off of her forehead.

"You came to the right place for help Kylie. It's time for a fresh start. For you and Billy. The team here will see that you get the help that you need. That is, if you are sure that you want it. But you're going to have to really want it. And it's not going to be easy. You must know that after where and how you ended up," I say to her squeezing her hand.

"I know," she says and nods as tears trickle down her gaunt cheeks. "I hit rock bottom. I'm so ashamed Brooke! So terribly ashamed. Everything spiralled out of control so fast that I didn't even know that it was happening to me. And poor Billy. Oh my God. Will he ever be able to love me again after this? And the kids. Do they know that I'm here?" she asks and pulls her hand away from me and then covers her face with both of her hands.

I pat her shoulder. I really hope that she has hit rock bottom and knows that it's over if she doesn't get help to stop the drugs.

"When the staff say that you're ready, you can ask Billy yourself. He's desperately wanting to see you. But please Kylie take this as a warning, a second chance because you're lucky to be alive. Listen to the team here and their recommendations for you. Give yourself that second chance. Don't you deserve that?" I say, and stroke her face again, worrying and wondering what will happen to her.

Can she do it? Will she do it?

I close my eyes. Please God, let her take the lifeline that's being handed to her. She's suffered enough. Please give her the strength to be able to do it. Suddenly, Lou Grimes' face flashes into my mind and my heart skips a beat.

I take a deep breath as my mind rushes to thoughts about Ryan. A tear spills out and snakes it way down my face before I can wipe it away. Ryan can't do it on his own. He didn't get a second chance!

Chapter Thirty-Four

"If you love me. You'll do it. For me Brooke. For us! For what we've always been. A team! A great team! Please Brooke. Don't forget. We had a deal! Remember," he said, squeezing my hands in both of his.

Unable to speak I remember that I just stared at Ryan. His plea was always the same. And he always used the same words to try to convince me.

"You're a doctor Brooke! You can start now and slowly stockpile the right amount for me. You know how to make the correct mixture for me to take. You can do it. Help me Brooke. You're my only hope out of this ordeal, this terrible dead end. Please promise me that you'll do it. If you love me, then you'll do it. You're my only hope Brooke," he had continued pleading with me over and over repeating the same words.

It was the night after we'd been to the neurologist and we'd seen the brain scans showing the lesions from his accident. He'd pushed his plate away and declined to eat any dinner and then he'd been pacing and refusing to get into bed. He got down on his knees and hugged my legs as I sat on the side of the bed.

"Please Brooke. If I was in a coma, useless on a DNR someone else would pull the plug. It only makes sense Brooke! I trust you! You can do it!"

"No I can't Ryan!" I'd said wiping away tears and pushing his hands away.

He'd grabbed on to my hands as I tried to stand up.

"I can't do it. I'd rather lose you to another woman. At least then you'd be alive and as horrible as that would be, well, I would rather have that," I'd replied terrified of what lay ahead for us.

I hadn't wanted to make the appointment with his specialist in the first place. But Ryan had insisted on doing it. He knew that he was starting to slide badly and I guess he wanted to be certain that there wouldn't be any turning back. That in the future there would be no improvement. That it could only get worse for him.

I've never been able to get the images out of my mind. The scans spelled disaster for him and for us as a couple. And the proof was in the fact that Ryan was having fewer lucid days and moments. That day had been one of his best days and it had been a devastating experience for him. Watching his reaction when the neurologist spoke was absolutely crushing.

He'd had a tight grip on my hands when he pleaded with me and his eyes were begging me to listen to him. He was squeezing so hard, but I didn't feel it in my hands. It was in my chest. It felt like he'd pulled my heart out and was squeezing it so tightly that I couldn't breathe.

"Promise me. Please. I'd do it for you Brooke! You know that. Give me the peace of mind that I need now. Let me go on knowing that you'll do it. Just one last thing for me. You can do it Brooke. No one will know. It'll be for the best. For you too. You can start over. You're young. You can find someone else. You can start a new life all over again. Please Brooke. Say that you will. Please! Promise me that you'll do it for me! It'll be our secret!"

I'd nodded. It was an automatic movement. Was I really nodding? Could I really do it?

"OK. I will. I promise," I'd said and then I burst into tears.

Ryan released my hands and grabbed me and pulled me up and hugged me tightly. We stood like that for several minutes. Tightly wound together.

He can no longer hug me back the way he used to. I tried to sit on his lap yesterday and it was impossible because he was so immobile. So instead I hunched down beside his chair and slowly unbuttoned his shirt and put my head against his bare chest. I kissed his chest, then I put my ear on his heart and listened to it beat.

People are meant to be together, not kept apart by anything, especially not by a disease of any kind. We need to touch each other and be touched in return. That's what makes us human.

"Don't forget our deal," was what he'd so often said to me throughout our marriage. I'd just smile and brush his words off not knowing what lay ahead for us.

But the strange truth is that he did say that to me so many times over the course of our marriage. I shake my head remembering him saying it sometimes just out of the blue, but always when we were feeling really close, after making love or after a dinner celebrating our wedding anniversary. Did he know? How could he know? Do people know these things? Do they have some kind of premonition about these big life changing catastrophic events? Is there a deep seated knowledge about potential disaster that lays waiting for us that is contained inside of our psyche in some kind of primordial way?

"If you love me..." his words constantly bounce around in my head echoing back and forth.

I'm in the kitchen. The sun is pouring in the window filling me with warmth. I finish mixing the juice. And I jump as the phone rings. I pull it out of my pocket and look at the screen. It's Kylie!

"Hi Kylie! It's great to hear from you. Yes we're home. I can't tell you how good it is to have him home for awhile. I told him that as long as we can manage, and I don't see why we can't with lots of help, for at least a bit of time, then he can be here in his own home. It'll be good for him. And for me too!"

"That's great Brooke. Were you able get the hospital bed that you wanted delivered in time?"

"Mission accomplished. It's here. I can manage him today and tomorrow by myself, and on Monday the 24 hour attendants start and that will obviously be a big help. We're going to have a great weekend together. Just the two of us. A final chance for us to be together again."

"Final?"

"Yes. Uh. You know, before the cycle of attendants begins. In and out. You know how that will be."

"Well, you sound so happy Brooke. This was obviously a good decision for both of you to have him at home for awhile."

"What about you Kylie. How is it going?"

She's back home after an inpatient stay in one of the best drug rehab centres in the country. We've only talked briefly a couple of times. But Billy called to say that things were going well so far and he was feeling cautiously optimistic.

"Good. It's good Brooke. Billy has been an incredible support. I really couldn't ask for a better husband. I'll be honest. I feel a little fragile, but I think this time that I have the tools I need to make it. To stay clean. If it's OK I'd like to visit you soon.

Just say when. In the meantime, don't forget that if you need anything we're here for you guys."

"I'm happy for you and Billy. And thanks Kylie. I'll talk to you soon," I say and put my cell down on the counter and walk to the bedroom with the glass of orange juice.

I enter the room and look at Ryan's favourite piece of art, a colourful abstract painting over the bed. My eyes tail down to look at Ryan. He's propped up with three pillows on the hospital bed with the rails up. There is no recognition from him that he knows it's me or even that there's someone in the room with him. He's just staring.

I smile at him and hover over him with the glass of juice. I hold it and help him drink from a straw.

When he finishes the entire glass, I remove two of the pillows so he is laying flatter on the bed.

I take the glass into the kitchen and wash it thoroughly with soap and water. Then I put it in the empty dishwasher and put it on the heavy cycle and press start.

I go back to the bedroom. I have some soft easy listening music playing. The kind we both always loved to listen to cuddled up on the sofa. I run my fingers over his face. His eyes are closed.

The room feels very still. It's tranquil. My body is calm. There's no anxiety. No panic. There's no more sadness in this moment. Only peace.

I sit down in the chair next to his bed and lean my head against the soft cushiony back of the large wing chair and close my eyes.

The sun coming in from the window behind me feels warm on my face and I think about the early days together when we were carefree. Carefree! Like in this moment, now! The realization jolts me and I blink and then fully open my eyes. I raise my head. The music has stopped. The room is quiet. No sound. I don't want to move. But I know that I have to move. I know that I need to call 911.

A shock wave rocks my brain. I turn and look at the bed. A moan erupts from my throat. I cover my mouth and take a deep breath. The ordeal is over! We kept our promise to each other. It'll be our secret forever.

I stand up and lean over his face and gently kiss him. We're bound together forever now!

" Goodbye my love," I whisper.

Constance Lechman
- AUTHOR -

"My novels explore the psychological forces and personal struggles that compel strong, successful characters to act in contradictory ways."

Constance Lechman is the author of six previous novels, Decisions, Options, Alternatives, Choices, Actions and Consequences.

A former social worker and health and social services administrator with master's degrees in social work and business administration, Constance has also published articles on psychotherapy and social work practice and research.

She lives in Montreal, Canada. You can connect with her on Facebook, Instagram, Goodreads and LinkedIn.

OTHER TITLES
by Constance Lechman

DECISIONS

OPTIONS

ALTERNATIVES

CHOICES

ACTIONS

CONSEQUENCES

MERAKI HOUSE
PUBLISHING

Publishing with Soul, Creativity & Love

Meraki House Publishing, founded in 2015 has established its brand as an independent virtual publishing house designed to suit your needs as the Author, delivering the highest quality design, writing and editorial, publishing and marketing services to ensure your success.

"Where your needs as an Author have become ours as an independent Publishing House."

WWW.MERAKIHOUSE.COM

In partnership with
www.designisreborn.com

Copyright 2020, Meraki House Publishing

Marnie Kay, Founder & CEO
marniekay.com

CPSIA information can be obtained
at www.ICGtesting.com
Printed in the USA
BVHW090302281120
594050BV00007B/19